SHADOWS OF GRAVEWOOD MANOR

A BEAUTY AND THE BEAST RETELLING

LAUREN SANATRA

Copyright © 2024 by Lauren Sanatra

All rights reserved. This copy is intended for the original purchaser of the book only. No part of this book may be reproduced, scanned, or distributed in any printed or electronic form, including recording, without prior written permission from the publisher, except for brief quotations in a book review.

This book is a work of fiction. Names, characters, places, and incidents either are products of the author's imagination or are used fictitiously. Any resemblance to actual persons, living or dead, events, or locales is entirely coincidental.

Editing Services: Cynthia Asmar

Cover Design: Hi_Logo Covers

Table of Contents

Prologue: Gregory 1
Chapter 1: Charlotte 5
Chapter 2: Charlotte 13
Chapter 3: Charlotte 19
Chapter 4: Charlotte 25
Chapter 5: Charlotte 31
Chapter 6: Charlotte 37
Chapter 7: Charlotte 45
Chapter 8: Graham 55
Chapter 9: Charlotte 63
Chapter 10: Charlotte 71
Chapter 11: Charlotte 77
Chapter 12: Charlotte 85
Chapter 13: Graham 103
Chapter 14: Charlotte 107
Chapter 15: Graham 113
Chapter 16: Charlotte 117
Chapter 17: Graham 123
Chapter 18: Charlotte 129
Chapter 19: Charlotte 135
Chapter 20: Graham 141
Chapter 21: Charlotte 147
Epilogue 151

Prologue: Gregory

The wind howled outside Gravewood Manor, its furious gusts battering against the stone walls, as if trying to tear the very house apart. Inside, the fire sputtered in the hearth, its flickering flames casting long, wavering shadows across the room. I sat slouched in a large leather armchair, glass of brandy in hand, my brow furrowed in a storm of my own making.

I'd been drinking steadily for hours. The amber liquid slid down my throat with each bitter gulp, dulling the sharp ache of my thoughts but doing nothing to soothe the crushing weight of my responsibilities. At twenty five years of age, I'd long since grown accustomed to the demands of my title, yet tonight, they pressed upon me with a merciless intensity.

Gravewood Manor, my ancestral home stood proud in the night, its windows dark and silent, as though even the house itself was mourning with me.

The blasted wedding, I thought bitterly. Lady Charlotte.

I had never met her. In fact, I hadn't the slightest idea what she even looked like. All I knew was that I was promised to her in marriage by a tedious arrangement of family obligations and social expectation. A woman I would have to marry whether I liked it or not. The very notion made me clench my jaw.

I stared into my glass, swirling the liquid absentmindedly, while the storm outside seemed to echo the turmoil in my chest. My mind, clouded with alcohol and frustration, began to wander.

She must be an absolute terror, or worse, some simpering fool who only wants to marry me for my title, my wealth, my place in society. It was the only thing that made sense.

I gripped the glass tighter. Why else would she be willing to marry a man she's never met?

I'd heard whispers from the ton about Lady Charlotte's beauty, or lack thereof, but to me, that seemed a trifling detail. She had sent me countless invitations to meet in person face to face, but like the stubborn bastard I was, I denied each one. What did it matter whether she was beautiful or not? She could be the ugliest woman in all of England, and I would still be bound to her by the invisible chains of societal expectation and my obligations that were set up by my parent's years ago.

Yet, somewhere deep down, there was an even darker thought, one that, despite my best efforts, kept creeping up from the depths of my soul. What if...

I shook my head, trying to banish the thought. *What if she's kind? What if she's sweet, and gentle, and trusting, and I destroy her?*

I could already picture it: her eyes full of warmth, her soft smile, her graceful movements. She could be full of hope and joy, someone who could see the goodness in me, despite the walls I had built around myself. And then, the misery that would follow when she realized the truth. But I knew it was too late. I could already see it, the disappointment in her eyes, the tears she would try to hide when she realized that I was not the man she imagined. That I was a shadow of what I should be, and she would be stuck with me.

SHADOWS OF GRAVEWOOD MANOR

I was a terrible man, a terrible duke, and I would make a terrible husband.

The brandy was gone now, and the gnawing discomfort in my chest remained. My mood darkened as I thought of the conversation I'd endured with my father's solicitor that very morning. The lawyer had reiterated that it was imperative that I marry soon. Society was watching, and the Hartwell name could not be left to wither without an heir. So the wedding was planned for the end of the year. *What was I going to do?*

I had done away with all my servant's weeks ago. I just wanted to be alone, so I ordered them out of the manor, their livelihoods shattered, but what else could I do? Every face in this house reminded me of my responsibilities, of the cold duty I had inherited, and I couldn't stand it any longer. The silence of the empty halls was all that was left to me now, and even that felt suffocating.

With a curse, I set the empty glass on the side table, stood with unsteady legs, and stumbled toward the door. "More whisky," I muttered to myself, my voice thick with frustration. "Perhaps that'll make it all go away."

The corridor was dark as I made my way toward the kitchen, each step echoing through the hollow expanse of the manor. The grand staircase loomed before me, its dark mahogany banister gleaming faintly in the firelight. I didn't care. I needed the whisky, the one thing that could perhaps still drown the endless thoughts that churned inside my skull

The flicker of my candle cast strange shadows across the stairs as I descended. My mind was lost in a haze, my limbs heavy with the effects of too much drink. My steps grew slower, less sure. A momentary dizziness struck, and then I moved too quickly, my feet unsteady, and I misjudged the first step. For a moment, I teetered, a brief, sickening sensation of falling, then—

The world tilted sideways. I flung my arms out in a desperate attempt to catch something, anything, but the railing was too far, and the stairs were too steep. My feet slipped out from under me, and I went down, tumbling in a blur of motion, hitting the cold stone with every jarring impact.

Each blow echoed through the stillness of the manor, my breath catching in my throat as I crashed onto the floor. My skull struck the stone with a sickening crack, and then a burst of light flared in my vision. It was as if lightning struck clear through the manor and into my body.

And then... nothing. The world fell away.

Chapter 1: Charlotte

The fire crackled softly in the hearth, casting flickering shadows across the room. Outside the window, the storm was building, heavy clouds rolling in from the west, the wind picking up, as though the very heavens were preparing for something ominous. Inside, however, the atmosphere was thick with a different kind of tension.

I sat by the window, my gaze fixed on the swirling snowflakes, each one unique, yet all destined to melt into nothing. *How fitting.* The faintest sense of dread curled in my stomach, growing with each passing moment. My father's voice, sharp and low, broke the silence.

"We've given him enough time, Helena." His words, though measured, carried a weight of frustration I hadn't often heard from him. "She's been engaged to him for almost two years now. Not a word from the Duke in months, hell it's been almost a year. You know how this reflects on our standing."

I stiffened at the mention of Gregory, the Duke of Gravewood, as my stomach clenched painfully. They didn't need to say it, I felt the weight of it in every breath I took.

It had never been a marriage for love, but for survival. A contract. A way to secure our family's future, to lift us from the deep pit of debt we had been sinking into for years. When the proposal or rather the agreement, had come a few years ago, I accepted, eager for the safety and security it promised. My parents had spoken of little else. I had accepted, but only because of the pressure that was pressing down on me from my parents.

"Perhaps we should write again," my mother suggested, her voice soft but edged with unease. She glanced up from the stack of letters, meeting my father's gaze. "Maybe he is simply occupied with his duties. The Duke has a great deal to oversee, after all."

"And perhaps he has simply lost interest in marrying a stranger," my father shot back, his voice sharp and biting. He clenched the letter in his hand, the last one we had received eight months ago, as if he might tear it into pieces. "I'm not a fool, Helena. You know as well as I do that a woman's value is often measured in the wealth and status of her husband. If Gregory thinks he can find someone with a larger dowry, we may very well be left in the dust."

The words struck me like a blow to the chest. I closed my eyes, feeling the oppressive weight of their expectations fall heavily upon me. I had known, deep down, that this arrangement was never meant to be about me. It was about survival. About securing our place in a society that measured worth by wealth, title, and connections. And I had accepted it, or so I had tried.

But now, months had passed since his last letter, and my family's mounting concern had only deepened. Their hope of financial salvation now hung precariously on the silence of a man I hardly knew, a man who had already shown a startling disregard for his promises.

SHADOWS OF GRAVEWOOD MANOR

I felt my mother's eyes on me even before I turned to meet her gaze. I knew the question she was about to ask, the one she hoped I could answer in a way that might ease the growing tension between them.

"Charlotte," she said, her voice a blend of hope and dread, "have you heard from him in secret? Has there been any word from the Duke since his last letter?"

I swallowed hard, the lump in my throat threatening to choke me. "No, Mother. Nothing."

My father's chair shot back with a jarring sound, as if his patience had reached its breaking point. He stood, his large form casting a shadow over the room. He was dressed in his usual dark suit, but it was his commanding presence that seemed to fill the room, making me feel small in comparison. The soft silk of my gown, a pale blue dress of muslin, its bodice tightly fitted and the skirt gently falling in soft folds, felt almost out of place in such a tense moment. The dress, though simple by the standards of many, still spoke of my family's decayed wealth, its delicate embroidery along the hem and sleeve cuffs a faded reminder of better days. My fingers tugged absently at the fabric, the cool touch of the fabric against my skin offering little comfort.

"This is intolerable. The marriage contract was signed months ago. His lack of correspondence is more than an oversight, this is a sign of disregard." My father's hands balled into fists, his knuckles white. "We cannot afford to wait any longer. We must take action."

I met his gaze, but the words I had intended to speak lodged themselves in my throat. The very idea of confronting Gregory, of writing to him again, pleading for what seemed like an afterthought to him filled me with a deep, sickening sense of helplessness.

"What do you suggest we do?" I finally managed, my voice unsteady.

My father's eyes narrowed, cold and calculating. "You must write to him again. Do not wait for another month to pass in silence. If he is too preoccupied to honor the engagement, then we will simply have to move forward without him before it is too late for you to find another. You need to plead for him to keep this contract."

A cold wave of anxiety rushed through me, mingling with the rising panic. I was not one to defy my father, his word was law, his decisions final. But the thought of putting myself in the position of begging Gregory to fulfill an obligation he had so easily discarded, of making myself small and insignificant, was unbearable. The very notion made my skin crawl.

"Perhaps," my mother suggested gently, her voice soft but coaxing, "you should write more personal letters, Charlotte. Appeal to his feelings. Make him feel your presence. Speak to his heart. Men are not always moved by duty alone."

I felt the heavy weight of her expectation pressing down on me, suffocating me. There it was again, the unspoken understanding that this marriage, this engagement was not about me. It was about duty and to save us from financial ruin. I was the pawn in this arrangement, and it was my responsibility to make it work.

But what if there was nothing I could do? What if Gregory had grown tired of his promise? What if the marriage was nothing more than a forgotten obligation?

SHADOWS OF GRAVEWOOD MANOR

I stood up abruptly, my chair scraping across the floor with a sharp sound, the sudden movement breaking the fragile silence. The pale blue fabric of my gown billowed gently as I pushed myself to my feet.

"I'll go," I said, my voice tight with resolve, each word cutting through the tension like a blade. "I'll go to Gravewood Manor myself."

My parents exchanged a look, one that conveyed both disbelief and concern. My father's brow furrowed as he looked at me, the flickering light from the fire casting shadows across his hard features. "Charlotte, that's preposterous. You cannot—"

"I can," I interrupted, meeting his gaze with a fierce, unyielding determination. The words that left my lips were foreign even to me, but they felt right. "If I cannot wait here for him to decide, then I will find out the truth for myself. I will not sit idly by while we wait for a man to fulfill an obligation he has already neglected. It is only a two days journey, or one if I ride through the night without a carriage to slow me down."

"You cannot travel alone," my father snapped, his voice thunderous. "The journey to Gravewood is treacherous at this time of year. And what of your reputation? What will people say if they learn of this? A lady of your standing cannot—"

"I am not a child, father." My voice wavered, but there was a steel edge to it now. "You cannot keep me confined to this house forever. I may not have been consulted on this engagement, but I will not live in uncertainty for another moment. I will go to Gravewood Manor, and I will see for myself if Gregory is still willing to uphold his end of the bargain."

"You are speaking of madness, Charlotte," my mother whispered, her face pale, as if the mere thought of such a journey would destroy everything they had worked for. "The journey is too dangerous, too far. And what would become of you if something were to happen? Think of the scandal! Think of—"

"I care not for the scandal," I said, cutting her off, my words sharp and unyielding. "What is the worth of a scandal, if it means preserving our dignity, our future? What is a reputation compared to the truth of what we have allowed to happen? No, Mother. Better a scandal than a life spent in waiting."

The room fell into a heavy silence. The crackling of the fire seemed to fill the space between us, but nothing could dissolve the tension that had solidified in the air. I could feel my parents' disapproval like a tangible weight pressing down on me, but I stood firm. This time, I would not be the passive pawn in a game I had not chosen.

"I am leaving," I added, my voice unwavering. "Tomorrow morning."

My parents exchanged a glance. My father looked at me as though I had suggested a most ridiculous thing. "Charlotte, that's preposterous. You cannot—"

"I can," I interrupted, meeting his gaze.

"No," my mother spat out. "You will write him one more letter, use your words to praise him and let him know you are ready to become his sweet and submissive wife." My mother was shaking now, "you need to show him you will not be an inconvenience for him but instead a dutiful wife."

Writing letters were getting me nowhere so far, I doubted this one would make a difference. My mother wanted me to be sweet and demure? Completely ready to get on my knees and obey my new master I would call husband. I really hope he wasn't like that or expected such behaviors from me. While I could easily play that part, I doubt I would be able to keep up that charade for the entirety of a life-long marriage.

"Fine," I hissed and marched back up to my room.

I sat at my window observing the still falling snow and I knew I had to take action. I could sneak out late in the night and ride straight for Gravewood Manor. By the time my parents realize I am gone, I will be half way there. It wasn't the best plan for a lady of my station, or any lady for that matter to ride alone and unaccompanied, but if I told anyone of my plans, surely they would blab to my parents and ruin it all. This would have to be a solo journey and I would not return until I had a few words with my future husband.

Chapter 2: Charlotte

I waited until the house had fallen silent, the glow of the hearth fading from the windows as my parents retired for the evening. The soft ticking of the clock in the hallway echoed through the stillness, reminding me that the night was slipping away, and with it, the chance to act. I had to leave tonight before the storm got worse. I just needed to wait a little longer.

In the darkened drawing room, I glanced toward the staircase, where my father's study was located just beyond the second-floor landing. My mother's voice had faded, muffled behind the closed door of her room. I could hear her soft breathing now, and my father's occasional cough, a sign that he, too, had finally settled.

It was the moment I had been waiting for and it was now or never.

With careful steps, I crossed the room toward the back door, my heart pounding in my chest. I couldn't afford to hesitate any longer. I had to leave. The pressure from my parents was suffocating, and I had to take matters into my own hands. It was the only way this whole thing could possibly go as intended.

I had spent months stewing in silence, wondering if the Duke had grown bored of the engagement or had simply forgotten about me. My mother's delicate suggestion that I write another letter and then another, this time more charming, that time more humorous, then another where I was completely fawning over him. Over this Duke I still hadn't met. But every letter stayed unanswered or was met with short and simple replies. That had only further buried the hopelessness I already felt. How could I bear to write another desperate plea? How could I expect Gregory to respond when, even in his last letter, there had been no hint of affection, only the cold formality of a man who did not know me?

No, I would not sit by and wait any longer. I would go to him. I would go to Gravewood Manor, where the answers might lie and then demand them from Gregory Hartwell. The Duke's lack of responses could not be explained away, not anymore. I needed to know why he was ignoring my letters and avoiding his obligation, and I needed to know *now*.

I reached the stables, where Raven, my black mare, was waiting for me. She didn't know it yet, but we were about to embark on an adventure. She shifted restlessly in the dim light, sensing my urgency. I ran my hands over her sleek coat, feeling the familiar warmth of her body. Raven was my only true companion in this. She was my constant friend in the solitude of the vast estate.

The wind howled as I slipped inside the small building and saddled her as quickly as I could. My hands shook from a mixture of cold and anticipation, but I pressed forward, determined.

I quickly gathered the things I would need. My thick riding cloak, my gloves, and a small satchel to carry a few provisions. It would be a quick turn-around trip that I hoped would end with a happily ever after, or at the very least an after.

SHADOWS OF GRAVEWOOD MANOR

The night air was bitterly cold, and the thought of the long ride ahead made me shiver. Taking one last look over my shoulder, I carefully unlatched the door and stepped into the cold night. The world beyond the house was draped in a thin blanket of snow which soon would become thick by the time I was able to ride back. The storm had picked up since dinner, and would probably continue to only get worse as time went on. The road ahead would be treacherous but it looked clear enough. It was now or never. Raven's hooves crunched over the fallen twigs embedded in the snow as I led her away from the stables, moving quickly but quietly towards the road.

I didn't want to be seen, not by the servants, not by anyone. If anyone knew I had left, my entire mission would be compromised. The idea of my mother's frantic search for me after she found the letter I left her on my dresser. The worry that would grip my father when he realized I was gone, made my stomach tighten, but I pushed the thoughts away. I had to focus on my mission and the task at hand.

I slid into the saddle, pulling the cloak tighter around my shoulders to shield myself from the wind chill that blew all around me. I gave one last glance at the house, half-hidden behind snow-laden trees, before I urged Raven forward, down the long driveway and onto the road.

The road to Gravewood Manor was a journey I had never made before. Though I had heard the name spoken in whispers among the townsfolk, and seen the distant spire of the mansion on the horizon when we traveled through the area, I had never had reason to venture so far. My parents' estate was far enough removed from the Duke's lands, and I had always been told that the road to Gravewood was dangerous, often abandoned during winter months. It would be frightening to travel alone, and yet, I had no other choice.

A part of me was thrilled to see my future home, well that was as long as things went according to plan. There was still a chance I would face rejection straight to my face by the Duke. We had never met or even seen each other. For all I knew he could be a ghoul or disfigured. That wouldn't bother me so much, as long as he had a good heart, but after his lack of personality he displayed in his letters, and now this, I wasn't sure if even that was enough for him to get by on. Perhaps he thought the same about me? I knew I was not the most beautiful girl in my circle, but I wasn't completely unfortunate. I had even caught the eye of quite a few men at a few social events, although I was unable to act. I was already engaged after-all.

My body frame with all the right curves in all the right places as my mother would say was one that even I was pleased with. My breasts; not too large but not too small. My long brown cascading hair against the pale of my complexion was one that society deemed to be a trait of beauty but for some reason, the gossip amongst the ton, was that I was just too plain. I didn't care. I may not have had all the best features but I did have a favorite, my hazel eyes. Many thought my eyes to be a bit too big for my face, but that's why I loved them. I was an emotional creature, most women were, but I loved that I could use only my eyes to tell someone exactly how I was feeling. I could flirt with a single bat of my lash, and I could smile with a single blink. They did betray me though on the days I was filled with sorrow and sadness, which were more often than not as of late. I was dreading marrying a stranger and every day that we got closer to the nuptials, were days that anxiety and sadness filled my eyes. But I had to do it, it was my duty as it was the Dukes.

After riding clear through the night and into the morning, it was time for a break. There were signs for a village that was close by and I figured it would be the best place to stop and get some sleep before continuing on. I urged Raven forward, her steps quick and sure as we moved through the thickening snow. The sun barely broke through the clouds, casting a golden glow on the snow blanketed earth, making the floor look like it was glittered with diamonds. The road twisted a few more turns winding and I could finally see the faintest outline of the village that appeared in the distance. *Thank God.*

There was a tavern straight ahead that offered rooms to rent and it looked like it was getting ready to open for the day. Having a drink this early in the morning was seen to be undignified, but as long as they were open and had a fire blazing, I couldn't judge.

The wind whipped harder, biting into my cheeks as I pressed on towards the tavern, ready to get some rest and warmth. The journey had been more difficult than I had thought it would be, but I was half way there and could not turn back now.

Chapter 3: Charlotte

My hands were numb from the cold, stiff and tingling with each small movement. The air was sharp, stinging me through the thin fabric of my gloves as I trudged forward. My breath came in ragged bursts, clouding the air before disappearing into the thick morning frost. Raven, her coat a dark silhouette against the pale dawn light, stood at the post outside the tavern.

The heavy oak door loomed ahead, dark and weathered, its brass handle gleaming faintly as the first rays of sunlight caught it. I pushed the door open causing the hinges to groan as I stepped into the warmth of the tavern.

A wave of heat enveloped me, wrapping around me like a blanket, and I inhaled deeply, savoring the rich smells that filled the air. Bacon sizzling in the kitchen, fresh bread just out of the oven, and the sharp, bitter scent of ale mingling with the earthy undertone of wood and smoke. I closed my eyes for a moment, letting the heat soak into my frozen skin, the fire crackling in the hearth almost a relief after the cold outside.

The tavern was far from crowded, given the early hour just a handful of men scattered at wooden tables, hunched over half-drunk steins of ale. Their voices were low, hushed conversations about business, life, or whatever it was they had planned for the day. But the speed at which they drained their mugs suggested none of their plans would see daylight outside these walls. I wasn't sure whether to feel comforted by their presence or uneasy about what their stares might mean.

I glanced quickly around the room, eyes darting to the bar. An older man stood behind it, grizzled and broad-shouldered, his thick hands polishing a mug with slow, deliberate motions. He didn't seem particularly friendly, but his eyes were sharp, scanning the room as though keeping watch for trouble. The tavern keeper.

I took a steadying breath and approached the counter, my footsteps muffled by the wooden floorboards. The unease in my stomach twisted tighter, but I forced my voice to remain even, despite the tension gnawing at me.

"Excuse me," I said, trying to ignore the rasp in my throat. "Do you have any rooms available?"

The tavern keeper looked up slowly, eyes narrowing as he took in my appearance, wet hair, travel-worn cloak, boots caked with snow. After a long moment of study, he grunted and slid a heavy mug of ale toward me.

"No thank you," I replied quickly, waving the offer aside. "I just need a room for a few hours. I'm looking for a warm place to rest before the storm hits."

His eyes lingered on me a little longer than I was comfortable with, and his thick fingers tightened around the mug. "A few hours, eh?" he muttered, then took a long swig, his gaze never leaving me. "You planning on staying longer, miss?"

I shook my head. "Just long enough to sleep off the cold," I said, my voice steady despite the gnawing feeling in my gut. "I'm headed out again soon, don't want to risk getting caught in the storm."

SHADOWS OF GRAVEWOOD MANOR

He studied me for a long moment, his gaze scanning over my face, then down to the worn edges of my cloak, the faint dirt on my boots. It felt like he was sizing me up, assessing my vulnerability. "You by yourself?" he asked, his voice low.

"Yes," I said, the word clipped, as though the answer were obvious. But I could feel his scrutiny, the weight of it pressing down on me. *Maybe I should have lied?*

His brow furrowed, and his voice dropped even lower. "Pretty thing like you, traveling all alone?" he said, his words almost a whisper. "That's dangerous."

I clenched my jaw, not liking where this conversation was going. There was something about the way he looked at me, something that felt like a question hidden in the back of his eyes. But I wasn't about to let him pry any deeper. I didn't need anyone asking too many questions.

"I'm headed to Gravewood Manor," I said, forcing my voice to remain calm, even though a small part of me recoiled at the thought of that forsaken place. "I'm meeting my fiancé there."

His brow furrowed even deeper, his eyes narrowing with confusion. "Gravewood?" He let out a low, almost disbelieving chuckle. "That place is abandoned. No one's been there in months."

My heart stuttered in my chest. *Abandoned?* That wasn't possible. It couldn't be.

"What do you mean, abandoned?" I asked, my voice sharper than I intended, the unease in my stomach spreading like cold fingers. "My fiancé lives there. He's the Duke, Gregory Hartwell. He's probably just—"

The tavern keeper's expression didn't change. His face grew even harder, his eyes dark with something I couldn't quite place. "Gregory Hartwell?" he repeated, as if tasting the name, then shook his head slowly. "Haven't seen him in months. The whole manor's been empty. Rumor is he's fled the country. You didn't know?"

I stared at him, frozen in disbelief. Months? Fled the country? I couldn't wrap my mind around it. The Duke of Gravewood didn't just disappear. He had responsibilities, he couldn't leave the estate, the workers, the people.

"No," I said quietly, more to myself than to him. "That's not possible."

His voice dropped, low and serious. "You should turn around, miss. I'm telling you, it's not safe to go there. The roads are bad enough, but the forest..." He paused, as if weighing his next words carefully. "There's nothing out there anymore. No one's seen anyone from Gravewood for some time now. I wouldn't go near it if I were you."

I stiffened, my back straightening as irritation flared inside me. I wasn't some helpless girl. "I'll be fine," I snapped, my tone sharper than I'd meant. "Now, how about that room?"

The tavern keeper didn't argue. With a grunt, he grabbed a key from a hook behind the bar and slid it across to me. "Up the stairs, second door on the left," he said, his voice soft but heavy with warning. "Get some rest. You'll need it."

I took the key and turned, my boots echoing softly against the floor as I made my way toward the staircase. The room at the top was small, barely big enough for the bed in the center and the solitary nightstand beside it. The bare walls were a dull gray, the air still and cold despite the fire downstairs. The shared bathroom was down the hall, though I had little intention of leaving the comfort of my bed for anything.

SHADOWS OF GRAVEWOOD MANOR

I hung my cloak on the door, the fabric brushing softly against the wood. The bed was simple, the blankets thin but warm enough for the short time I would be there. I collapsed onto it, burying myself beneath the covers, trying to hold onto the warmth of the tavern, but the chill from the conversation with the tavern keeper clung to me, gnawing at my thoughts.

I closed my eyes, desperate to sleep even for just a few hours then I would be on my way to figure out what was going on with Gravewood Manor as well as my betrothed.

Chapter 4: Charlotte

After only a few hours of sleep, I felt recharged enough to continue the journey. The snow had begun to drop more aggressively leaving no room for me to sleep another minute.

I retrieved Raven and we set off towards Gravewood Manor. We had to make it by nightfall or there was a good chance we could get stuck out in the storm and there were no nearby towns I was aware of close to the manor. We had to make it or risk freezing to death, and then what would become of my family?

After hours of non-stop riding, the sun began to set as a blanket of stars began to paint the sky. The cold chilled my flesh as I clenched my cloak tighter around myself. My hand became achy and numb from holding so tightly to the reigns. "Almost there girl," I said to Raven who must have been as cold and tired as I was.

We reached the forest that surrounded Gravewood Manor and it was here that the paved road ended and the forest path began. A makeshift path was embedded throughout the trees as I was sure many carts and carriages forged their own way through the thick forest. It was hard to see in the dark, but I let my instincts guide me as much as possible.

Hope flickered through my body as I could see the edge of where the forest ended. Ahead in the distance I could make out the shape of a large home, Gravewood Manor. We had made it. As Raven and I made our way down the long, winding path to the manor, the wind howled like a living thing, tugging at my cloak and stinging my face with icy shards of snow. Every step was a battle against the elements, but I couldn't stop now, not when the answers I needed lay just beyond the thick, iron-gate.

The manor was straight ahead, a dark silhouette against the gray sky. The place was vast, far grander than I had expected even blanketed in the dark. From what I could make out through the driving snow, it looked ancient, as if it had stood there for centuries, untouched by time, and yet somehow decaying, as though the manor itself were giving in to the elements.

I dismounted from Raven, my legs stiff from the long ride, and led her toward the back of the manor to scout out for a stable. Raven, too, seemed eager to find shelter, her hooves clattering against the frozen ground as we neared the stable. I could barely make out the shape of the barn through the dark or the growing storm, but the familiar shape of the stable door was a welcomed sight.

The heavy wooden door creaked as I pushed it open. There were no other horses stationed inside, only the scent of damp hay and aged wood filling the air. Raven shook off the snow that clung to her coat, eager for warmth, and I quickly unlatched her saddle, smoothing my hand over her wet coat as I secured her in the stall.

"Stay safe, Raven," I whispered, though I knew she wouldn't answer. But her soft, snort was enough to soothe my nerves.

I turned toward the manor again, my breath misting in the cold. The wind howled louder now, carrying with it the scent of old wood and wet earth, mixed with the sharp tang of pine from the surrounding forest. The scent clung to my skin, making me shiver as I stepped back out into the storm. The back door of the manor loomed ahead and I made my way towards the icy steps.

To my surprise, the door was unlocked. I paused, glancing back over my shoulder, but there was nothing. No sign of life. No welcoming lights shining from the windows. Nothing but the oppressive dark and the ever-growing storm. I pressed the door open, the old wood groaning in protest as it swung open. A cold draft rushed out to meet me, and I stepped over the threshold.

The entryway was dimly lit by flickering sconces that cast long shadows across the stone walls. The air was frigid, the temperature inside no better than it had been outside. Dust hung thickly in the air, a fine, powdery film that coated everything in sight. Along the walls I could see the faint outline of where portraits once hung but were now absent. *What happened here? The* innkeeper was right. This whole place looked abandoned and forgotten.

I hesitated for a moment, taking it all in. This place, this grand but decaying manor, felt *wrong*. It was as though it was left to rot. It was clear no one was living here and maybe this entire trip was for nothing. There was no sign of life, no servants or staff bustling about, just the weight of silence hanging heavy in the air. The atmosphere was thick with it, like a presence in the room, pressing down on me. A cold dread crept up my spine, the hairs on the back of my neck prickling. I felt as if the house was watching me. Something felt wrong here. Wrong and tragic.

I passed under a set of large, gilded mirrors that reflected the pale light, their edges cracked and tarnished. The glass shimmered faintly as I walked past, distorting my reflection just enough to make my skin crawl. I could almost swear I saw something shift in the glass, too quick to catch, before it returned to normal.

I shivered but not from the cold. Something really felt off about this whole place. How long had the Duke been gone? Had he simply moved or disappeared from society somewhere in the woods? Or had he really fled England?

The hall seemed to stretch on forever, endless doors lining either side. I came to a set of stairs, the banister carved in intricate patterns. The staircase spiraled upwards into darkness, and I could feel the weight of the stillness pressing in from all sides. The steps groaned under my weight as I ascended, and I had to move slowly, carefully. The snow that clung to my boots began to shake off onto the steps as I climbed up.

I continued up until I reached the top floor. My gaze went from one door to the next, wondering which rooms lay beyond them. The silence was overwhelming. There was no laughter, no sound of footsteps or voices, not even the quiet murmur of a clock ticking somewhere in the distance. Just emptiness.

I began to pry open each door, trying to figure out which one belonged to the Duke. Maybe there was a clue about his absence or even his whereabouts. I did not come all this way to leave empty handed, there had to be something to explain all of this.

I was about to open the last door at the end of the hall and then I heard it. A haunting sound. It sounded like a rustling, a whispering, as if the very walls themselves were sighing. The whole thing was unsettling, causing unease to fill my tense muscles.

Get out...

My heart skipped a beat. I froze in place, every muscle tensed a bit more as my skin filled with goose pimples. I whipped my head around, but there was nothing, nothing but the darkened corridor and the shadows clinging to the corners of the rooms. The whisper felt so real, so near.

Get out... leave this place...Now!

The voice seemed to echo in my head, a warning, a command, but I couldn't tell if it was real or just an illusion from my lack of warmth and rest. All of a sudden a vase from the hallway flew clear across the room, shattering against the wall nearly missing me. My pulse quickened, my breathing became shallow. I turned to leave, my feet moving quickly toward the staircase, eager to escape the manor that seemed to close in all around me.

But then it happened. My foot slipped on the now-melted snow I left behind on the steps. The floor beneath me shifted suddenly, and I felt the world tilt dangerously. My arms flailed to try and catch myself, but it was no use. The old wood beneath me was slick with melted snow, and before I could regain my balance, I lost my footing completely. My body pitched forward, and I heard a sickening crack as my head collided with the hard, unforgiving stone floor.

I groaned in pain, my eyes closed tight. As I opened one eyelid at a time I saw the outline of a dark figure hovering above me that made my heart race. I wasn't sure if it was due to the pain or the fear, but suddenly I couldn't breathe. I felt my eyes roll back and the world went black.

LAUREN SANATRA

Chapter 5: Charlotte

I awoke with a start, a sharp pain shooting through my skull as I tried to sit up. The dizziness hit me first, then the realization that I was no longer lying on cold stone, but something soft. A bed. My fingers instinctively moved to my head, where the bruising from my fall made my skin throb.

"Easy there." A low, gravelly voice drifted to me, filled with a mix of amusement and something that felt almost like irritation. "You've taken a nasty knock to the head."

I turned my head slowly, my eyes widening when I saw the man standing by the door. He was tall, broad-shouldered, with hair that was dark but touched with lighter streaks of blonde, as though the sun had kissed it long ago. His face was rough, the kind of face that looked like it had seen a hundred winters despite him probably only being a few years older than I. His eyes were dark brown, almost black in this light. Wary eyes that seemed to take in every detail of me with unnerving precision.

I froze, suddenly aware that I was alone with a man, a stranger. *A man who had just found me unconscious*, and now I was lying in his bed. My heart stuttered with a burst of panic.

"Wh—where am I?" I stammered, clutching the blanket beneath me like it could somehow protect me.

He raised an eyebrow, his lips pulling into something between a smirk and a frown. "You're in Gravewood Manor.

Where else would you be?" His tone was blunt, no warmth, no concern in his words, only a trace of exasperation. "You hit your head, miss. Hard. Figured you wouldn't make it much farther."

My breath hitched as I quickly glanced around the room. The fire crackled softly in the hearth, casting flickering shadows across the room. The bed was cozy, the room simple yet well-kept, far from the bleak, cold atmosphere of the manor's entryway. But there was something unnerving about it all. Something about being here, in a stranger's house with a strange man, alone.

"You... saved me?" I asked, still unsure how I felt about being in his care.

He looked at me for a long moment before answering, "I didn't save you, miss. I found you. There's a difference. And now, you're here because the storm's too fierce to leave. So you can either rest, or you can argue with me. I'm not particularly interested in the latter." His tone was dismissive, and there was no softness in his words. It was almost as if he was annoyed that I was injured. That my presence was a burden to him. *Then why help me?*

I straightened in the bed, my back rigid. "I need to leave. The storm—"

"You're not leaving tonight." His voice was firm, with a finality that made me feel uneasy. "It's far too dangerous. Unless you want to freeze to death outside, then be my guest."

I tried to ignore the sting of his words, but it was difficult not to feel like a nuisance. Still, I wasn't about to back down. "I can handle a storm," I muttered, though I wasn't entirely sure of it myself. Although facing the storm might be a walk in the park compared to this stranger's company.

"I'm sure you can," he said dryly, his eyes flicking over me. "But you're not going anywhere in that condition. Rest here, and when the storm clears, I'll show you out."

His bluntness hit me like a slap in the face. "I—"

"Look," he interrupted, the frustration in his voice growing. "I didn't drag you in here for my health. I'm not about to let you die because you think you're some kind of hero. Trust me I don't want you here anymore then you want to be either. Just rest and wait out the storm. And if you still want to leave tomorrow, then you can go. If you are on a suicide mission, I won't stop you."

I frowned, growing more irritated with every word that left his mouth. "I'm not some helpless woman," I said sharply, my pride pushing me to challenge his assumption that I couldn't take care of myself. "I don't need your charity."

He eyed me as if I'd just said something incredibly foolish. "I didn't offer you charity, miss. I did what anyone would do when they find someone with blood dripping from their head unconscious on a cold stone floor. You must really think me to be heartless if you thought I would just let you bleed out and freeze to death. Most people would say thank you."

I let his words sink in and he was right. He could have just left me there and my blood would have frozen quicker then it could puddle onto the stone floor. "Thank you," I said reluctantly.

"You're welcome."

"So can I at least know the name of my reluctant savior," I said sarcastically.

He leaned back against the doorframe, crossing his arms. "I'm Graham, I look after the manor as the groundskeeper while it's been vacant, and you are?"

I forced my expression to remain neutral, even though my heart was still racing from the awkward tension. "I'm... Charm," I said quickly, before I could stop myself. I wasn't sure if I should give away my true identity in case this *Graham* turned out to be some sort of charlatan. I was after all a girl with a known name in high society, even if no one knew my family's financial situation.

He raised an eyebrow, as if sensing something off about my tone. "Charm? Is that your *real* name? Seems a bit odd, don't you think?" he scoffed a cruel laugh. "Not that it's my business." He shrugged nonchalantly, clearly uninterested in digging deeper into my story.

I didn't respond, my eyes flicking away. The last thing I needed was him knowing who I truly was. The Duke's fiancée? No. That would only complicate things.

"I suppose it was because my parents hoped I could charm society in some way," I argued, just a bit offended by his opinion of my name, even if it was a fake.

"And did you?" He asked cynically.

"No," I dryly replied as I got ready to deliver another lie, a lie I hoped would earn me some information regarding the Duke. "I am a maid for the Willow family, I was sent here to learn why Charlotte Willow's fiancé, Gregory Hartwell, has just disappeared leaving her engagement and arrangement with him unsettled."

Graham's face turned cold, "The Duke?" he questioned.

SHADOWS OF GRAVEWOOD MANOR

"Yes," I said, "My lady was due to marry him soon, but there has been no word from him in months. I was sent here to confirm his whereabouts."

"I'm afraid he's gone miss. Up and left a few months ago with no timeline on when he was planning on returning, I was hired to take care of the manor in his absence."

Gone? He just up and left? *No no no no*. I needed him, needed this marriage to bind us or else my family and I would be homeless and starving soon. "What do you mean he just left? He has an obligation to my lady—"

"Consider the engagement now null and void," Graham said without a shred of sympathy in his voice. "I'm sure a girl from such a prestigious family can find a new suitor, one she was not forced to marry in any sort of arrangement."

"Is the Duke that much of a scoundrel that he could not have told her this in person, or even by letter!" I shouted, causing the pain in my head to throb.

"Yes," Graham said bluntly. "Yes he is, tell your lady it is time for her to move on."

Everything was falling apart. I knew when I came here there was a chance I would be rejected by the Duke straight to my face, but now? He has just disappeared with no excuse or reason why he would break this contract. The idea of coming home empty handed and letting my family down made me sick to my stomach. I was a pathetic girl who went chasing after a man I never even met, ready to beg him to marry me.

"Are you ok, miss?" Graham asked, "Please do not vomit all over those sheets, they are the last of the clean ones in the manor."

This man was so cruel without an ounce of compassion in him. It would serve him right to make a mess of the fabric only so he would have to go out of his way to clean it. Although with the storm brewing outside and my head still throbbing, there was no telling how long I was actually going to have to remain here. I would need a clean and warm blanket to make it through the chill that ran throughout the manor.

"If he is truly gone, then I will be leaving first thing in the morning, storm or no storm," I declared. "If not I am sure people will come looking for me."

"With a storm such as this, all roads have surely been snowed over by now. Only those with a death wish would travel this far north."

"All the more reason for me to leave now to spare them the journey." I crossed my arms in defiance.

"And the injury to your head?" He asked with suspicion.

"I'm already feeling better," I lied. I had to get home and inform my parents of this news immediately. Maybe Graham was right and I still had time to find a respectable groom. It would be to another man I wouldn't have the time or luxury to get to know, but I was already prepared to marry a stranger as it was.

He glanced over his shoulder at me, his expression unreadable. "I'm sure you are," he muttered sarcastically.

"So it's settled," I said, this time quieter to ease the pounding in my head. "I'll be leaving tomorrow."

Graham didn't respond. He just turned and walked out, leaving me alone in the dimly lit room with nothing but the sound of the storm outside to keep me company.

Chapter 6: Charlotte

The wind howled outside, its fury crashing against the walls of the manor like a relentless beast. The storm had only grown worse since Graham left me to recover and I hated that he was right. I was stuck in this room, but I had refused to lie in that bed all day. After all, I wasn't some delicate flower that needed to be coddled and treated like a fragile doll. It was just a small bump on the head. I could handle the pain.

With my head still aching, I carefully made my way across the room, my feet soft against the polished wooden floors. I found the large window looking out over the estate, its view obscured by thick, swirling snow. The sight was both beautiful and terrifying.

I had no idea how long the storm would last, but I wasn't about to wait around all day. The thought of being trapped here any longer, even under his watch, was unbearable. I needed to come up with a back-up plan for my upcoming marriage and I had to come up with it quick.

"Charm?"

I spun, my pulse quickening at the sound of his voice. Standing in the doorway, Graham leaned against the frame, arms crossed, a scowl firmly in place.

"You're up." He eyed me with something like surprise mixed with frustration. "You should be resting."

"I am resting," I said sharply, forcing myself not to sound as defensive as I felt. "Resting my mind. The bed's too confined."

He raised an eyebrow at that, clearly unconvinced. "Is it?"

I swallowed, feeling the weight of his gaze on me. "I need to stretch my legs. A few steps around the room won't kill me."

Graham sighed, clearly uninterested in an argument but unable to suppress his annoyance. "You're lucky I don't lock you in here before you go wandering around like a fool and take another spill." His eyes darted toward the window behind me. "You see that?" He gestured to the storm outside. "It's not getting better. Therefore you unfortunately will not be leaving anytime soon."

I was growing increasingly frustrated with his overbearing attitude. "I'm not a child, Graham," I snapped, feeling the heat of irritation rise in me. "I can decide when it's safe to leave, not you. I'm not asking for permission." He made it very clear he did not want me here any longer then I had to be, so why was he starting an argument about it?

He rolled his eyes, muttering something under his breath about women and their stubbornness, but there was a flicker of something more behind his irritation. Maybe it was concern, or maybe it was just the weight of responsibility he carried. But I wasn't about to let him decide my fate.

"If you freeze out there, then it will be on my conscience. Selfishly I would like to live guilt free without worrying about if your leaving would result in your demise. Therefore, you will stay here until it clears up and then I will happily send you on your way and out of my life."

He was right, and I hated admitting to that. I would never make it more than a few miles, not to mention poor Raven having to navigate us through the storm. I was stuck here.

"Fine," I reluctantly said, crossing my arms. "So," I said, shifting the topic to distract myself from my growing frustration. "What exactly do you do here as the groundskeeper?" The house looked like it had been neglected for so long reflecting on Graham's work here or rather lack of such things.

His face darkened slightly, and he unfolded his arms, stepping into the room. "I look after the place. The manor, the fields, the stables, the whole lot of it. It's hard work, especially in the winter."

"I see," I said, a small flicker of amusement in my chest. "A man of many talents. A keeper of grounds, a caretaker of souls."

His gaze snapped to mine, sharp as ever, but this time there was a ghost of a smile tugging at the corner of his lips. "I wouldn't call it that," he muttered. "Though sometimes it feels like it. More trouble than it's worth, to be honest."

I couldn't help but chuckle. "Sounds like you're stuck with more than you bargained for."

"Well unlike a lady such as yourself, I am used to a bit of hard work."

I rolled my eyes, "Do you always talk to your guests like this, or am I just lucky?"

He huffed, looking away with a slight scowl. "Guests? I don't get many of those. Most people avoid this place like it's cursed, even when the Duke was here. And I can't say I blame them."

At the mention of *cursed*, I stiffened. "What do you mean? You said the storm keeps people away, are you saying no one visits the Duke?"

Graham shot me a sharp glance, his expression unreadable. "That's right. Not many people make their way out this far, especially not in weather like this. As for the Duke, he was a grumpy bastard who avoided people like the plague and in turn they avoided him."

I raised an eyebrow, intrigued despite myself. Did I perhaps get lucky with having the Duke leave? Was he really that unbearable to be around? There was a story there, one that he was clearly reluctant to share. The air between us grew heavy, but before I could press him further, he spoke again.

"You shouldn't be wasting your time asking questions. You're still not in any condition to be out of bed."

A sharp retort died on my tongue as I tried to suppress the urge to snap at him. Instead, I merely folded my arms and looked away, feeling the familiar sting of frustration building inside me.

"So, when you found me," I said, trying to shift the conversation back to a safer subject, "how did you know I was in the house?"

He hesitated before answering, his gaze flicking toward the window again. "I was out checking the stables as I heard the sound of an animal present while going out for some firewood. As the Duke took all of his horses with him, I knew it had to be a stranger looking for refuge. When I returned to the manor I heard something clatter down the steps, and then, I saw you lying there, half-conscious realizing it had to have been you making such a ruckus. Couldn't just leave you there."

SHADOWS OF GRAVEWOOD MANOR

I frowned, feeling a wave of gratitude mixed with uncertainty. "Why help me? You didn't have to."

His eyes darkened slightly. "Do you really think I would be so cruel and heartless and leave you on the floor to die?" He paused for a moment, as if something about my expression had softened his demeanor, even if just slightly.

"Well, then," I said after a beat, my voice lighter to break the silence. "I suppose I should thank you again for not letting me freeze and bleed out to death."

He grunted, his expression unreadable. "Just don't get any wild ideas. Like I said, I'm not interested in keeping anyone here longer than necessary."

I nodded, holding his gaze for a moment before turning toward the fire. We fell into a kind of awkward silence, neither of us quite sure how to navigate this strange, forced proximity. The storm raged outside, its fury louder now that we were inside, and I couldn't help but feel like I was trapped in the middle of it, not just by the storm, but by the tension with this strange man who seemed to want nothing more than for me to leave.

Minutes passed, and I could feel Graham's eyes on me, though he didn't speak. I looked up from the fire and met his gaze, catching the slightest flicker of something in his expression. Frustration? Resignation? Or something deeper?

"Well," I said after a while, breaking the silence again. "I suppose I should be grateful for your hospitality, then. Even if you seem dead set on getting rid of me."

He smirked slightly. "Don't mistake my *hospitality* for kindness. It's just practical. Like I said, I don't let people die if I can help it. I can't say the same about keeping them around for any longer than necessary."

The words hurt more than I expected, but I simply nodded. "Understood. But you're not rid of me just yet, it seems."

A flicker of something, amusement, perhaps, crossed his face, though he quickly masked it. "Seems not. Though I'm not sure if that's a good thing or not."

"So," I began slowly, "Am I truly to be confined to this bedroom only?"

Graham didn't answer right away, as if he were trying to think of a way to meet me in the middle. "You may explore the manor, but you may not go outside."

"What about the stables?" I asked, remembering I had left Raven there. "I need to check on my horse."

"I have already done so and she is fine, well fed and warm," Graham said dryly. "But if the storm calms down, you are permitted to go as far as the stable to visit her, but no further, especially not the far side of the property."

"Why," I asked like a child pestering their parents. I could be a brat if he was going to be an ass.

"It's too close to the woods where all sorts of dangerous creatures lay waiting for a fresh meal."

The idea of being mauled by a wolf or a bear sent shivers down my back. "Ok," I promised, "I won't go past the stables."

Graham nodded and quickly exited the room. The exchange felt like a small victory. Though I had no idea what this storm and strange encounter would bring, I knew one thing for certain: I needed to proceed with a backup plan and quick, but I wasn't going anywhere just yet.

SHADOWS OF GRAVEWOOD MANOR

Chapter 7: Charlotte

The next morning I awoke feeling much more like myself. It seemed as though Graham left me a plate of what looked like some stale bread and a glass of water. I guess there wasn't much of a reason to keep fresh food in the manor with it being vacant aside from Graham himself. He probably was hoarding all of the good food for himself. I was lucky he left me anything I suppose.

I took a small walk around the room to warm up my muscles from being bedridden per Graham's orders. He was right though, if I wanted to leave as soon as possible, I needed to let my body rest and heal. It seemed to have worked as I was feeling much better now.

I glanced out the window and the snow storm looked as though it was taking a small break. It still didn't look safe enough to travel, but it was getting there, or so I hoped.

Scanning the grounds, I saw the outline of a house on the far side that led into the woods. The glass of the structure reflected off of the sun that was eagerly beaming down. It was a greenhouse I was sure of it. From here it did not look too far, and I was willing to brave a small walk in the snow if it meant there was a possibility of fresh crops growing in the greenhouse. It was near the far end of the property, the area Graham did not want me to visit, but surely the greenhouse was safe. Otherwise why have it where it was located if there was a fear of losing your life each time you had to go grab fresh food. I hoped it still had fresh vegetables. I could easily steam them as I had seen our kitchen staff do back home. The meal would be a much better alternative to the dry stale bread that my stomach was still trying to digest.

I grabbed my cloak and tucked it snuggly around my body to prepare myself for the cold. Hopefully Graham was occupied with some sort of project around the manor that he wouldn't see me slipping out. When I returned with the fresh vegetables I was sure he would have figured out about my small adventure on the grounds, but I would have to apologize with some freshly cooked vegetables. It was the least I could do after he had saved me and then looked after me. I would make him a nice warm lunch, a sort of truce between us. He could hardly be mad at me after that, especially after I could prove I was able to come back in one piece.

I poked my head out of my room and scanned the halls. No Graham in sight. I tiptoed down the creaky wooden stairs and headed towards the back door and out into the elements. It was still freezing outside, but not as bad as the night I had arrived. I tracked through the snow towards the greenhouse like a woman on a mission.

REACHING THE GREENHOUSE, I opened the door and stepped into its warmth. It wasn't as warm as my room in the manor, but it was warm enough for the vegetation growing within to thrive, well sort of. There wasn't much around. A carrot patch, some heads of lettuce growing, and even some radishes. I noticed a small garden barely surviving in the corner. It consisted of a few wild flowers and even fewer white roses. They were beautiful, but my mission here was for food not flowers, and I would take what I could get.

I found a basket that must have been left inside to harvest and began to pick away at the surviving vegetables. It was barely enough for a solid meal, but it would have to do.

Holding the basket tight beneath my cloak as the wind began to pick up, I rushed quickly to the snow, craving the warmth or rather the warmer temperature of the manor. I glanced back at the woods that began behind the greenhouse and a cold chill ran through my body. There was something that felt as if it was pulling me towards the direction of the woods behind the greenhouse. My body felt as if it needed to explore further like there was something waiting for me out there. I shook my head trying to erase the thoughts and forced myself to walk back towards the manor.

I ENTERED THE MANOR and found the kitchen. It too looked as though it had not been touched in months. Maybe Graham was also subject to the taste of the stale bread? I would change that. I would make him lunch. A gesture, simple and perhaps a little foolish, but a gesture nonetheless. A thank you for taking care of me when I had fallen ill, for offering me shelter when the storm had turned the world outside into a ruthless, frozen wilderness.

I was able to get a small fire going to boil some water. As I set the basket on the counter and began pulling out the vegetables, slicing them with quick, practiced motions, my mind drifted briefly to Graham. He was a strange man, distant, brooding, and at times, inexplicably cold. Perhaps he was more than just a reluctant caretaker, more than just the man who had allowed me to stay here, but I wasn't sure if I wanted to unravel the mystery of him. For now, I would keep busy. I would make lunch and show him that I was capable of taking care of myself and play the role of the maid that he believed me to be.

I was deep in thought as I chopped, the knife cutting through the vegetables with rhythmic precision. The sound of the chopping echoed off the walls, a strange comfort in the otherwise eerie quiet of the manor.

That was, until the unmistakable sound of boots crunching on the floor broke the silence. My heart leapt in my chest.

I turned just in time to see Graham enter the kitchen, his gaze cold, stormy. The tension in the air thickened, and I could feel the heat of my own face flushing with a mix of nerves and irritation.

"What the hell do you think you're doing? Where did you get those?" His voice was low, furious, a growl that made the hair on the back of my neck stand up.

I blinked, taken aback by the intensity of his anger. "I—" I began, but he didn't give me a chance to finish.

"What were you thinking?" he demanded, stepping forward, his eyes flashing with fury. "You *left* the house. You think it's safe to go running around to the far side of the grounds in this weather, all by yourself? What did I tell you about the woods there?"

I froze, the knife still in my hand. His words cut through me like the sharpest blade, and for a moment, I couldn't speak.

SHADOWS OF GRAVEWOOD MANOR

What had I done wrong? Was he really that angry that I left? But I was here, and I was ok, no harm done.

"I—I went to the greenhouse," I stammered, trying to defend myself. "I was just getting some vegetables to make lunch. For you. To thank you for taking care of me."

His face twisted with frustration, and he clenched his fists at his sides. "Thank me? By nearly freezing to death in the middle of a storm or getting mauled by a wolf? Are you completely out of your mind? How far back did you go?"

I stood there, stunned, holding the knife loosely in my hand. "I only went as far as the greenhouse I swear. I didn't think it would be such a big deal," I whispered, more to myself than to him. "I just wanted to do something. You've done so much for me."

His laugh was short and bitter, devoid of any warmth. "You're *thanking* me by putting yourself in danger? I don't need you to risk your life just to make me a damn meal."

My chest tightened, and I couldn't stop the surge of frustration that bubbled up inside me. "I'm not some fragile, helpless child, Graham. I can make my own decisions. I can take care of myself. I thought you might appreciate a small act of kindness in the dreary place."

His face reddened with a mixture of anger and something else I couldn't quite place. He took a step closer, his boots scraping across the stone floor, his voice rising. "You don't know anything about this place! You don't know what could be lurking out there, waiting for some fool to wander off into the storm. Do you think it's just *pretty snow* out there? You think you can just stroll outside without consequences?"

I shook my head, fighting to keep my voice steady. "You're overreacting. I'm fine. I'm perfectly fine. I've survived worse."

"You *don't* understand," he snapped, his words like a slap. "You think you're some heroine, but you're not. You're *alone*. You're at my mercy, Charm, and you need to remember that. You think you can just waltz around here as if nothing's wrong, but you're *wrong*."

I flinched at the venom in his voice. The weight of his words hit me like a heavy stone. *You're at my mercy.*

"I'm not your prisoner," I said, my voice barely above a whisper. "I never asked for any of this."

The words hung in the air, thick and oppressive. We stood there, staring at each other in the silent tension that filled the room, neither of us willing to break it. His jaw clenched, his fists still tight at his sides.

Finally, after a long, tense silence, he exhaled sharply, stepping back, though he didn't quite look at me. "I'm not asking for your thanks, Charm," he muttered, "and I'm not asking you to *thank me* by throwing yourself into danger you foolish girl!" Graham finished, his body vibrating with rage.

"It's just vegetables—"

Before I could get another word out, Graham suddenly grabbed the basket filled with the remaining vegetables and threw it across the kitchen. "You will obey me!" he screamed. "I gave you one rule and you broke it!"

I stood there for a long moment, the room feeling too small, too suffocating, the air thick with unspoken words. The forage lay forgotten on the counter and now on the floor, my carefully crafted meal now seeming utterly meaningless. I felt a sudden burst of frustration, sharp and stinging, welling up inside me.

I didn't want to stay in this house, not with him, not after that.

Before I could stop myself, I marched to the door, pulling it open with force. The cold hit me like a slap across the face, but I didn't care. I wanted to be outside, away from the man who thought he could control me, who thought he could treat me like a child.

"Where do you think you are going?" Graham moved to stop me.

"To the stables!" I screamed back, "I would rather be in Raven's company then yours, she's at least civilized."

"Then go!" Graham shouted so loud his voice sent echoes through my body.

I stepped outside, slamming the door behind me as hard as I could. The snow was coming down harder now, thick, heavy flakes swirling through the air. I pulled my cloak tighter around me, but the wind still cut through, sharp and biting.

I didn't look back. I just walked through the thickening snow, my boots crunching against the frozen earth. My breath came in quick, angry bursts as I made my way toward the stables. I reached the door and pulled on the handle, expecting it to give, but it was locked.

I tried again, panic rising in my chest, but the door refused to budge.

I spun around, my heart pounding, and dashed back to manor's back entrance as the snow began to fall more violently. If I couldn't get into the stables, the next safe place would be the greenhouse. I swallowed my pride and decided going back to the manor was more sensible and safer now that the snow had picked up since my last visit.

I would have to admit defeat and lock myself away in my room to wait the rest of this storm out and then take my leave. I would slip back in quickly before Graham could give me an *I told you so* sort of speech and head straight to my room.

I pulled on the back door of the manor, but it remained in place as if it were frozen shut.

Suddenly, the reality of it hit me: I was locked out. That bastard locked me out! He did tell me to go, but I didn't think he would actually lock me out!

A surge of frustration coursed through me. "Graham!" I shouted, my voice lost in the howling wind, but there was no answer.

I pounded my fist against the door. "Let me in!"

But the wind stole my words, and the cold seeped into my bones. The greenhouse was now my only option. The air grew heavy with snow flurries and I could no longer see the direction of the greenhouse. *No no no no.* Was it to the left? Straight ahead and to the right? I couldn't remember.

I banged on the door again, pain shooting from my frozen fist. "Graham please!" I shouted, but the cold was freezing me from inside out, causing my vocal chords to become raw and hoarse. I was trapped outside. After all his talk of not wanting me to freeze to death, yet here I was. I saw a pile of old wood to the side of the manor and crawled under it as a makeshift shelter and bundled myself under the cloak. I felt my heart beat start to slow as my whole body became numb.

I was going to die out here, and it was all his fault. *No, it was my fault.*

SHADOWS OF GRAVEWOOD MANOR

Chapter 8: Graham

I hadn't meant for things to go like this.

The anger, the harsh words I'd thrown at her, it all seemed so small and inconsequential in the face of what had happened. I hadn't meant for her to be out there, lost in the snow. But that's what I had done. I'd pushed her, scared her off, told her to go, and now she was nowhere to be found.

The minute she stormed out, I felt my body go numb. I had to find her.

The storm outside howled with a vengeance. Snow was falling so thick I could hardly see my own hands in front of me, much less make out any form in the vast white expanse. I forgot I had locked the stables and it seemed she had figured that out. *But then where did she go instead of there?* I called her name, though I knew it was futile. The wind swallowed the sound, but still, I called her, hoping against hope that she could hear me, hoping she would be huddled somewhere, waiting to be found.

I rushed to the greenhouse to see if perhaps she decided to go there upon learning the stable was locked, but there was no sign of her. I didn't know when the fear had crept in, but now that it had, it was relentless, gnawing at me. Charm couldn't be out here for long. The storm was cruel, and I had been crueler, dismissing her and letting her leave off into the bitter cold. If anything happened to her, I wouldn't forgive myself.

God help me, I thought. *Please let her be alright.*

I pushed through the snowdrifts, my boots sinking deep into the cold earth, making each step harder than the last. The wind cut through my coat like a blade, but I didn't stop. I had to find her. I *had* to.

And then, when I thought I needed to give up and accept her fate, I saw her.

Her dark figure was barely visible in the midst of the storm, slumped under a pile of wood by the back door. I must have rushed right past her without even looking, wasting precious time as I was sure she was freezing to death with each passing minute. I felt my heart lurch, panic rising up in my throat as I hurried toward her, my legs aching with each step.

"Charm!" I called out, my voice strained, desperate. I reached her, my hands trembling as I knelt beside her. She was unconscious, her body unmoving, and I could see the telltale signs of the cold already setting in. Her lips were tinged blue, her face pale and slack.

I couldn't think. I just acted. Without hesitation, I scooped her up in my arms, my heart hammering as I felt the unnatural cold of her body seeping through my coat. She was lighter than I'd imagined, too light, as if the cold had already begun to drain her strength.

I couldn't waste another second. I rushed back to the manor, not caring about the snow or the storm, only her.

Please, please don't be dead. I couldn't lose her due to my cruelty and temper.

I was out of breath by the time I finally reached the top of the stairs, but I didn't stop. I kicked the door open to the room I had laid her in from before, as it was the warmest in the entire manor, the fire in the hearth still crackling only barely. My mind raced with panic.

She was cold. Too cold.

I laid her down on the bed, my hands still shaking as I tried to cover her with a blanket, praying the warmth from the fire would help. I started the fire up again, stoking the embers with my bare hands, desperate to get some more heat into the room.

Her breathing was shallow, and her skin felt like ice against mine.

"Charm," I said softly, my voice thick with fear. "Please wake up. You have to wake up."

It took longer than I expected, but finally, after what seemed like an eternity, her eyelids fluttered open. I couldn't breathe for a second, just watching her struggle to focus, her eyes blinking slowly like she wasn't sure if the world around her was real.

"W-what happened?" Her voice was so weak, barely audible, but it was a sound I welcomed nonetheless.

"You're alright," I said, trying to keep my voice calm even though my heart was racing. "You're safe now. You're inside."

Her lips twitched as if she wanted to speak, but she was still so unsteady, so drained by the cold, that she couldn't manage more than a faint smile.

"Safe," she repeated weakly, her eyes soft but distant. "You say that like it means something."

I exhaled a sharp breath and leaned in closer, my voice dropping to a whisper. "It means everything to me."

I didn't know why I said it. It just came out, unbidden, a raw, desperate confession. But her smile faded, and she closed her eyes again, drifting in and out of consciousness as I tried to keep her warm, wrapping blankets around her fragile form.

I couldn't just let her slip away.

I couldn't lose her.

'Then why did you lock me out," she said weakly. "I banged on the door and called for you to let me in, but you never came." A stray tear fell from her eyes and it killed me.

She called out for me? I must not have heard it over my own anger that was brewing in my head. Or was it that empty numb feeling that overcame my senses when she left? She could have seen what was behind the greenhouse, the very secret I was trying to hide.

"I did not hear you, I swear. And as for the door, with the cold the metal must have frozen the metal locks into place. You must believe me, seeing you in pain is the last thing I want." And that was the truth. I wasn't sure how or why I felt so protective over Charm, but it was a feeling that started developing the moment I saw her lifeless body on the stone floor of the manor. That moment made everything so real for me.

"I thought you were angry with me and that's why you—"

"No," I stopped her before she could say more as I saw another tear about to roll down her pale face. "Even in anger, I would never wish somebody harm, least of all you."

Charm just nodded and I hoped she had understood that it was an accident. That I was no longer angry but scared. Scared of what might have happened to her if I was too late in finding her. "Please get some rest, I will bring you something warm to eat and drink when you awake, but for now please sleep."

I stayed at her side, my thoughts a blur of guilt and worry. *I did this. I made her leave. She wasn't supposed to be out there.* But now, all I could do was wait for her to wake up and hopefully forgive me. She was alright, and she was safe.

WHEN HER EYES FINALLY fluttered open again, she looked at me with a weary expression, and this time, I could tell she was more lucid. I leaned closer to her, brushing a strand of damp hair from her forehead.

"Feeling better?" I asked, not sure what else to say as I handed her a mug of warm tea. The tension in the room felt thick, and the weight of everything that had happened hung heavy between us.

She gave a weak nod and took a sip from the mug. "I suppose so. You just scared me with how angry you got."

I felt my face become strained with guilt. "I know, and for that I am sorry. My temper can overtake me sometimes, it's been like that for as long as I can remember."

She rolled her eyes as she continued to sip on the warm tea. "Excuses, excuses," she said teasingly.

I couldn't help but chuckle, though the sound was strained. "Can you forgive me?" I asked, hoping her little jest meant that she was no longer scared or angry with me.

She let out a sigh, her eyes softening. "I suppose I have to, considering that was the second time you have saved my life."

I stood, brushing the dust from my coat not knowing what else to say considering I was the one who put her in danger in the first place. "Would you like something warm to eat, you must be starving. I finished steaming those vegetables you so kindly gathered and added them to a soup."

She shifted slightly in the blankets, her eyes slowly focusing on me. "You cooked for me, after all that?"

"Consider it another part of my apology."

She began to sit herself up, her face flushed with warmth from the fire. I handed her a bowl of soup I'd managed to put together, the scent of broth and herbs filling the room.

She took the bowl with a half-grin. "I don't suppose I'll get any more angry glares with this, will I?"

"I'm still angry that you went out there on your own," I replied, sitting down across from her, my own bowl in hand. "But I'm less angry at you now. You've got the whole *half-dead thing* going for you."

She snorted, shaking her head, but her eyes softened. "I'll take that as a compliment."

And for a few moments, we just ate, the fire crackling between us, the storm outside forgotten in the warmth of the room. But the tension was still there, an unspoken understanding that hovered between us.

After a while, I stood again, not knowing exactly why I felt compelled to do it. "I'll clean up," I muttered, ready to escape the quiet, unsure of how to deal with the fact that the weight of her near-death experience had put something new in the air between us. It made me feel as if I would disappear if she didn't pull through. But she was going to be ok now, I would make sure of it.

"Don't go," she said softly, her voice almost vulnerable.

I turned, startled.

SHADOWS OF GRAVEWOOD MANOR

Her gaze was steady, and her lips curved in a soft, hesitant smile. "Stay," she added, her voice almost a whisper.

And for a long moment, I just stood there, caught between the flickering light of the fire, the silence, and the storm outside. I didn't know what to say, so I said nothing and stayed.

Chapter 9: Charlotte

The storm had passed overnight, leaving a pristine blanket of white over everything. The world outside the manor looked like a painting, each tree branch weighed down by snow, the earth smooth and untouched as if waiting for something to disrupt its stillness.

I could feel the warmth from the fire lingering in my bones, the thick woolen blankets Graham had wrapped me in still clinging to me, though I'd long since discarded them. My head no longer felt foggy, and the dizziness that had plagued me for the last few days had faded.

I hadn't realized how much I'd missed feeling *well*, how much I'd taken it for granted until I'd been on the brink of losing it all. The cold, the fear, the storm, it had all felt like something out of a nightmare, and now that I was awake, it was hard to believe how close I had come to losing myself to it.

As I sat by the window, gazing out at the snow-covered grounds, I couldn't help but feel a sense of peace, even after almost dying twice, and even after learning about the Duke leaving for good, leaving me and my family in a very hard spot. But for now, none of it mattered.

Graham appeared in the doorway, and the moment I saw him, I realized just how much I'd missed his company. I wasn't sure what it was, whether it was his gruff manner or the way he always seemed to be in control of everything, but there was something comforting about his presence. Even now, standing there with his sleeves rolled up and the firelight catching the edges of his tousled hair, he was the anchor I didn't know I needed.

"You're looking better," he said, his tone flat, but I could see the flicker of something softer in his eyes. Something like relief, or maybe concern? I wasn't sure.

I smiled at him, pushing myself up from the chair. "I feel better," I said, feeling the truth of it in every movement. "I think I'll survive."

"The storm seems to have passed, so if you feel well enough, it should be safe for you to travel back home." Something like sadness flickered in Graham's dark eyes.

"Do you want me to leave?" I found the courage to ask, feeling like something was sparking between us these last few days. Truth be told, it would crush me just a little if he still wanted my presence here gone. I wasn't sure I was ready to leave yet.

"You are a grown woman Charm," Graham said while he straightened up his posture. "You can make up your own mind about such matters, I will not stop you."

I thought about this and it felt like maybe this was an olive branch. I liked that he was going to let me decide for myself, but I was too stubborn to admit I was enjoying my time here with him. "I think it would be better if I stayed a little longer, just to be sure the storm has fully passed."

He raised an eyebrow, the corners of his mouth twitching as though he might say something, but then he simply nodded.

"Good. Because I was thinking it might be a good day for a little fun. If you are up for it?"

I cocked my head, eyeing him with suspicion. "Fun?"

Graham's lips curved into a grin, the first one I'd seen in days, and it was so unexpected that I almost didn't recognize it. "Yes, fun. You've been cooped up in here long enough. I thought we might go sledding."

I blinked, confused for a moment. "Sledding?"

He shrugged, a mischievous glint in his eyes. "I'm not sure how well you'll handle it, but there's a hill behind the manor that's perfect. As long as you're feeling up to it."

"Feeling up to it?" I repeated as I eyed him. "I just got over a near-death experience, and you want me to go sledding?"

He chuckled. "You mean to tell me you braved a day's journey alone by horseback through a snowstorm and a little sledding scares you?"

I couldn't help but laugh, the absurdity of the situation catching up with me. The Graham I had met initially had been all cold eyes and sharp words. This version of him, the one standing before me, was something else entirely, lighter, teasing even.

"I suppose I could give it a try," I said, a playful edge creeping into my voice. "But don't expect me to go easy on you if I wipe out."

"Wipe out?" he said, a deep, sarcastic laugh escaping him. "That's *exactly* what I'm hoping for."

WE MADE OUR WAY OUTSIDE, and the snow glittered in the pale light of the morning. I breathed in deeply, the crisp air filling my lungs, and felt the weight of everything from the past days start to melt away.

As we walked, Graham's hand hovered near mine, like he wasn't sure whether he should touch me or not. I couldn't say why, but I noticed it. And I felt my pulse quicken just a little.

Finally, we reached the sleds, which were stashed behind the stable. They were the old-fashioned kind, wide enough for two, with thick leather straps and a sturdy frame.

Graham grinned as he pulled one from the stack. "Hope you're not afraid of a little speed, Charm." His voice had a teasing quality to it, but there was also something protective in the way he looked at me.

I stepped up to the sled, eyeing it with a mix of excitement and nervousness. "I don't think I'm afraid of anything, except maybe your temper," I shot back, giving him a smirk.

He raised an eyebrow, clearly amused by my challenge. "You're *really* going to give me trouble after what happened the other day?"

"Well," I said, brushing a few snowflakes from my coat, "if I'm going to freeze to death again, I'd like to at least have some fun before it happens."

He laughed, a full, rich sound that warmed the air around us. "You have a strange sense of humor."

"I'll take that as a compliment," I replied, and he shot me an amused look as he positioned the sled at the top of the hill.

We climbed onto the sled together as Graham positioned himself in front of me. The cold nipping at our exposed skin, but the thrill of the moment made everything feel alive. As we pushed off, the world seemed to fall away, the wind rushing past my face, the ground flashing beneath us in a blur.

I could hear Graham's voice muffled by the rush of the wind. "Hold on tight."

We flew down the slope, the sled bouncing and skidding over the snow, and I couldn't help the laugh that escaped me. The whole world felt like it was narrowing to this moment, this insane, exhilarating ride with Graham at my side.

When we finally came to a stop, my heart was racing, and I realized I was grinning, breathless and giddy.

"That was..." I didn't even have the words for it.

Graham looked at me, his lips parted as if he were going to say something, but then the words seemed to fade. For a moment, there was only the silence between us, and the sound of our breaths mingling in the cold air. I could feel the heat of his gaze on me, but there was something else there, something different, something that made my heart skip a beat.

We continued to repeat the process over and over again. We would climb the slope, I would sit behind him, my grip tightening with each journey down the hill, and we would fly.

"Can I steer this time?" I pleaded.

"And have you crash us into a tree?" He answered playfully. "Haven't you had enough near death experiences to last you a lifetime?"

I rolled my eyes, but my smile didn't falter. "You're just jealous because you think I will be better at than you."

He raised an eyebrow, clearly amused but not about to let me get the last word. "Better, huh? I bet you had your eyes closed the whole time when we were racing down that hill. Your fingers were practically digging into my stomach with how tight you were holding on to me."

I blushed, whether from the cold or from the implications of his words, I wasn't sure. "Maybe I just wanted to hold you close?" I said without thinking and immediately regretting it.

He chuckled softly, but then his expression shifted, becoming more serious. "I should have known you'd be trouble."

I tilted my head at him, confused by the sudden change in his tone. "What does that mean?"

His gaze softened for a moment, his lips parted like he was going to say something. Was he going to tease me about my accidental comment?

And then, before I could make sense of it, he looked away, his eyes shifting as he abruptly stood up. "Come on. Let's go back inside. We're wasting daylight."

I stood, too, though I was left staring after him, trying to piece together the feelings that had stirred up between us. He'd almost said something. *Hadn't he?* But the moment had passed.

The walk back was quieter, and though we exchanged a few more words about the snow and the hill, the energy between us felt different.

What was that? I wondered, my heart still fluttering in my chest like a caged bird. There had been something between us, something unspoken, but I wasn't sure what it was. Was it just the thrill of the sled ride? Or was there something more?

I glanced over at Graham, but he wasn't looking at me. His expression was unreadable, distant even. I couldn't help but wonder if I'd just missed my chance to ask him about it.

The thought left me with a sinking feeling in my chest, but I didn't know how to push through it. I had no idea what I was

SHADOWS OF GRAVEWOOD MANOR

feeling, and I was starting to think I might never understand what he was feeling either.

The rest of the day passed in a blur of silence between us, the tension from the sled ride still hanging in the air, unanswered. I was no closer to figuring out what it meant, what we meant.

And maybe, just maybe, I wasn't ready to.

Chapter 10: Charlotte

The evening passed quietly, almost too quietly.

Graham had made a simple dinner, just a pot of leftover soup and some bread, but it was more than enough to fill me, especially after the cold air from the sledding. I'd noticed he didn't say much, which was typical for him, but there was something more distant about his silence tonight. His gaze kept shifting away from mine, and I couldn't tell if it was because I was still here and he truly wanted me gone, or if something else was on his mind.

We ate in the small dining room, the flickering candlelight casting shadows on the walls as I sipped my broth. There was something between us now, something that hung in the air and I wasn't sure if I was excited about it or terrified. He wasn't someone I could marry let alone be with. Not when I had a financial obligation to my family and I was still relying on the Duke to follow through. I shook my head trying to erase those thoughts.

When we finished, Graham didn't offer to keep me company as I had expected. He simply stood and cleared his plate.

"Good night," he said, his voice low but polite, his eyes avoiding mine again.

"Good night," I replied, feeling the awkwardness of the exchange settle like a weight between us.

He turned to leave, but then stopped at the door, his back to me. "Don't go wandering off again," he added, almost gruffly, though I could sense the faint worry behind his words. "I won't be chasing after you if you get lost."

I smiled despite myself. "You're right. I've had enough adventures for one week." He nodded without looking back and left, and I was left alone with my confusing thoughts and emotions.

The sound of the wind outside had picked up again, but the storm had died down. The house was still, except for the occasional creak of wood or the whisper of the fire. It felt as though the house was watching my every move and at first it terrified me, but now I was intrigued.

It was a strange sort of peace that settled over me as I prepared for bed. But even as I lay under the heavy covers, trying to calm my racing thoughts, I couldn't shake the lingering tension from earlier. I didn't understand what was happening between me and Graham. What it was, or why it was there, but I felt it. He went from being such a cold stranger to someone I would even call a friend. It was evident that he cared about me in some capacity, but I was still unsure if it was due to him not wanting to feel the guilt and responsibility for me if something bad happened, or if it was true feelings of concern. I had hoped it was the latter.

Every time our eyes met, my heart fluttered just a little faster. Every time he spoke, I heard something more than just words, something like longing, or regret, or maybe... *want*.

SHADOWS OF GRAVEWOOD MANOR

But I couldn't be sure. He had pulled away before anything could happen, and now I was left with the strangest feeling of wanting, mixed with utter confusion. My thoughts kept returning to the way he looked at me after the sledding, like he was on the verge of saying something. Something important.

But neither of us said it.

I rolled over in bed, staring at the ceiling, wondering if I would ever understand the strange, stirring feeling that churned inside me. I should've been thinking about my family, about the mess I had been sent here to clean up. But instead, all I could think about was Graham. I closed my eyes tight to allow sleep to take me away from all of this confusion.

I woke up to the sound of screaming. The kind of scream that rips through the air, raw and unrestrained, and sends a chill down your spine. *Was it a ghost?* The one I swore I heard the night I arrived?

My heart lurched in my chest. I froze for a moment, wide-eyed and confused. It took me a second to realize it was coming from somewhere close and familiar in the manor. It was coming from the room across from mine in the hall. It was coming from *Graham's* room.

I quickly threw off the covers and rushed to the door, my heart thumping so loudly it almost drowned out the scream. I tiptoed across the dark hallway, my feet silent on the cold floors. The only light came from the flickering lanterns by the stairs, casting long shadows that made everything feel strange and eerie.

When I reached Graham's door, I hesitated. The scream had faded, but the sound of frantic movement inside had not.

He was in distress, his muffled mutterings growing louder. I swallowed hard and, without thinking, pushed the door open.

Inside, Graham was thrashing around in the bed, his hands clenched into fists, his body trembling. The blanket had slipped off his chest, leaving him half-exposed, his face twisted in terror. I focused my eyes on his half naked body and I realized my sleepy eyes must have been playing tricks on me. He was shaking so bad it looked as though he was coming in and out of focus. Something was wrong.

"Graham," I whispered, but he didn't hear me. He was lost in whatever nightmare was plaguing him.

I hesitated, unsure of what to do, but my feet seemed to move on their own. Before I knew it, I was at his side, kneeling by the bed, my hand gently touching his shoulder.

"Graham, wake up," I said more firmly this time, shaking his shoulder. "It's just a dream."

His dark eyes snapped open, wide and wild with fear. For a moment, I thought he might strike out at me, but when his gaze landed on me, the terror in his eyes softened. He blinked a few times, as if trying to make sense of my presence.

I quickly pulled my hand away, heart racing, but he didn't push me away. He just lay there, staring up at me, his breath still ragged.

"What happened?" I asked, my voice soft and filled with concern.

For a long moment, he didn't answer. His lips trembled, his eyes darting to the side as if he couldn't quite meet my gaze.

"Nothing," he muttered, but the tightness in his voice said otherwise.

SHADOWS OF GRAVEWOOD MANOR

I didn't press him. Instead, I sat beside him on the edge of the bed, unsure of what to do next. I reached for the blanket and pulled it up over him, my fingers brushing his skin in the process. The contact sent a shock through me, and I pulled my hand back quickly.

"I... I'm sorry," I said, not really knowing what I was apologizing for. "I didn't mean to wake you."

Graham let out a long breath, sitting up slowly. He ran a hand through his hair, his face still pale. He glanced at me again, but this time there was something vulnerable in his eyes that I hadn't seen before.

"You don't have to apologize," he muttered. "It's not your fault."

I was about to say something else, but then I saw the look on his face, the way his eyes seemed to drift closed as if he was too tired to even stay awake. Without thinking, I slid under the covers next to him. I couldn't just leave him. I wanted to comfort him and ease his worries.

His body was tense, but I could feel his muscles slowly relax as I inched closer. The bed was wide enough for us both, but the closeness between us felt different than it had before.

"You want to stay?" he asked softly, his voice a rasp. He wasn't looking at me, but I could tell he wasn't pushing me away either.

I didn't answer. I just curled up beside him, my body instinctively drawing closer to his warmth. His bare chest was both rock solid and soft as silk. Slowly, I let my head rest against his chest, my breath evening out as the last remnants of fear from the nightmare slipped away.

For hours, we lay there, neither of us saying a word. The only sounds in the room were the crackling of the fire and the occasional gust of wind outside. I could feel Graham's steady heartbeat beneath my ear, a rhythm I hadn't noticed before but now felt oddly comforting. And despite the chaos of my thoughts, the confusion, the questions, I felt a strange sense of peace. For once, I wasn't worrying about the future, about the obligations that had brought me here. I wasn't thinking about Gregory or the marriage that had never happened.

All I could think about was the warmth of Graham's body next to mine, the steady rhythm of his breath, and how it felt to simply *be*. I still didn't know what this was between us. I didn't know where it was going, or what it meant. But I knew one thing for sure, nothing had ever felt more *right*.

Somewhere in the quiet of that night, as I drifted off to sleep, I realized that maybe I didn't need to understand everything. Maybe I didn't need to have all the answers. Because, right then, I only cared about being here, with him. And that was enough.

Chapter 11: Charlotte

The first thing I noticed when I woke up was how warm I was. Warm in a way I hadn't felt in days, like the chill of the snowstorm had finally left my bones. I was cocooned in soft, thick blankets, the kind that made you feel like you could sleep for a hundred years. My head was resting on something firm, but warm, Graham's chest, I realized with a jolt.

I quickly sat up, my heart pounding but the bed was empty beside me now. The sheets were still rumpled from our restless sleep. For a moment, I wondered if I'd imagined the whole thing, the way I'd curled up beside him, the way he hadn't pushed me away. The comfort, the peace of that strange, intimate moment.

But no, it was real. I could still feel the warmth of his presence lingering in the room, his scent faint in the pillows and sheets. I wrapped the blanket tighter around myself and glanced toward the window. It was still early. The light from outside was soft, the world still wrapped in layers of snow, the morning mist clinging to the trees.

Graham was nowhere to be found.

I swung my legs over the side of the bed, I hesitated for a moment, still feeling the heaviness of sleep in my limbs, before standing up. As I walked down the hallway, I could hear movement, quiet, deliberate sounds. Curious, I followed the noise.

I found him in the hall, his back to me, his head bent as he focused intently on something. His sleeves were rolled up, and his shirt was untucked, as usual, but there was something oddly endearing about the way he was going about it. He was standing on a step ladder, a broom in his hand, carefully reaching up to clean out the cobwebs in one of the upper corners of the ceiling.

"Graham?" I called softly, not wanting to startle him and have him fall from the ladder.

He didn't turn at first. But when I stepped closer, I saw a brief flicker of surprise cross his face before he schooled it back to his usual nonchalance.

"Morning," he said, looking down at me. There was a faint smile on his lips, but it was more of a small curve than anything that could be called a grin. Still, it made my heart skip in a way I wasn't quite ready to acknowledge.

"What are you doing?" I asked, still wrapped in the blanket like a makeshift robe. "Cleaning cobwebs?"

"I told you I was the groundskeeper and it's my job to take care of the manor," he replied with a shrug, his focus still mostly on the broom in his hands. "It's about time it looked presentable again. I wouldn't want a beautiful lady like you stuck in a depressing, cobweb-ridden house."

The compliment was so unexpected, and so blunt, that I almost didn't know how to respond. My cheeks heated, and I shifted awkwardly, trying to cover up my reaction.

"A beautiful lady?" I repeated, arching an eyebrow. "I'm just a maid, remember? A foolish maid." I finished with a little sass.

SHADOWS OF GRAVEWOOD MANOR

He finally turned around, his expression earnest but with a playful glint in his eyes. "It's the truth, and you're not *just* a maid. I was wrong to call you foolish before and I apologize. But this place is just..." He paused, glancing around the dusty hallway, the light catching the edges of the forgotten corners. "Sad. Empty. But since your arrival it seems to have come back to life a bit."

I stood there for a moment, processing his words. There was something in his voice that made me soften. The place *was* a little sad, unloved, uncared for. But hearing Graham apologize and acknowledge it, hearing him want to fix it on behalf of the life I seemed to breathe back into the place. It felt oddly sweet, like he was trying to make it better for me, for both of us.

"Well, you're not wrong," I said finally, my voice light, teasing. "It's not exactly too cozy in here."

He chuckled, the sound low and warm. "Yeah, well, it'll do. But I think it deserves more than this miserable atmosphere."

I couldn't help but smile, watching him for a moment. His hair was a mess, like it always was, and his shirt had a smudge of dust on it from the ceiling. But there was something charming about how seriously he took the cleaning, as if it were a task of the utmost importance.

"You're really going to clean the whole manor?" I asked, a smile tugging at the corner of my mouth.

"Why not?" he said, his mouth quirking up slightly. "Someone has to do it, it was why I was hired after-all."

"I'll help," I offered, stepping closer, still wrapped in my blanket. "It's the least I can do."

He looked at me, his brow furrowing, though there was a hint of amusement in his eyes. "You're sure? You're not going to go running off exploring and get yourself lost again?"

"I'll stay close," I promised. "Besides, you can't possibly do all this yourself. I'll help with the cobwebs."

Graham gave me a skeptical glance. "Cobwebs? You?"

I shrugged. "I might surprise you. I am a maid for the Willow's after-all."

"Don't get your hopes up. I'm not going easy on you just because you're a lady, maid or not," he said with a half-smile, his eyes glinting with that mischievous edge. "This is real work."

"Well, I *am* a lady," I said with mock seriousness, "and I'm prepared to do this properly. Don't think you're getting away with doing all the hard work."

He snorted, shaking his head, but he handed me the broom with a reluctant smile. "Alright, Charm. But if you break something, I'm blaming you."

I took the broom with exaggerated grace, holding it like it was a scepter. "Of course. I'm a *perfect* lady. I would never break anything."

"You're already making me regret this," Graham muttered, turning back to his own task. "If you break the chandelier, I'll be the one having to fix it."

"Noted," I replied, swiping the broom at the nearest corner. The webs came down easily, though I might have been a little too enthusiastic about it, as the broom swished too low and nearly knocked over a small vase on a nearby table. I would never pass as a real maid. Hopefully he didn't already see through my lies.

SHADOWS OF GRAVEWOOD MANOR

"Careful!" Graham warned, catching the vase just in time, but the look he gave me was filled with something like amusement. "I knew this would happen."

"Hey!" I protested. "It was *almost* a disaster. I saved it. A true lady never leaves a job unfinished."

He rolled his eyes but grinned. "A lady, huh? A *very* enthusiastic lady. Don't make me take your broom away."

We worked in silence for a while, but the air between us was light, filled with small moments of laughter. Every so often, he'd give me a playful nudge or tease me about the way I held the broom too dramatically, and I'd shoot him a look, telling him that he clearly hadn't seen the way *proper* ladies maids cleaned.

We moved from room to room, cleaning windows and sweeping corners, bantering the entire time. At one point, I knocked over a candle, and he lunged forward to catch it, his hand brushing against mine in the process. For a moment, neither of us said anything. There was only the quiet hum of the house, the sound of our breathing, and the strange, undeniable pull between us. My breath caught, but I quickly broke the silence with a laugh.

"Clumsy me," I said, pulling my hand back.

"You're full of surprises," Graham replied, his voice a little rougher than usual. "I didn't expect you to be actually *good* at this."

"I'll have you know," I said with mock seriousness, "I'm quite skilled at cleaning. It's one of my many talents in the Willow's manor."

He smirked. "I see. Let's just hope you don't turn the whole manor upside down while you're at it or the Duke will be furious with me when he returns, or rather if he returns."

I had almost forgotten about the Duke and in this moment I truly did not care when or if he returned at all. The only thing that mattered was this moment now.

By the time we had finished, the house had started to feel like a different place altogether. The rooms no longer felt dusty and forgotten. There was a warmth to them now, a new life in the walls, and I couldn't help but feel a little proud of what we had accomplished together.

As we stood in the main hall, hands on our hips, surveying our work, I couldn't stop the grin from spreading across my face.

"Well," I said, "it's not *perfect*, but it's definitely better."

Graham nodded, his lips curling into a satisfied smile. "Yeah, I'd say so."

We stood there for a moment, the air between us thick with an unspoken tension. Neither of us dared to voice it aloud. Slowly, Graham reached up and tucked a stray lock of hair behind my ear, his fingers brushing against my skin in a quiet, intimate gesture.

"I guess I owe you one," he said softly, his voice almost a whisper. "Thanks, Charm."

I smiled up at him, but the words I wanted to say stuck in my throat. "You're welcome, Graham."

And for the briefest of moments, the world seemed simpler. No marriage contracts, no debts hanging over us, just him, me, and the quiet satisfaction of a job well done.

SHADOWS OF GRAVEWOOD MANOR

"So," Graham began, breaking the stillness, "tell me about your lady. Lady Charlotte, was it?"

My stomach clenched, an uncomfortable knot forming as his words lingered in the air. "What would you like to know?" I asked, my voice coming out slower than I intended.

"She was supposed to marry the Duke, right? What's she like?"

Ah, here was my chance. The opportunity to sell myself, to let the Duke know exactly what he'd missed out on. Maybe when Graham saw him again and explained how foolish the Duke was for missing out on this opportunity, he'd regret walking away. Or at least, reconsider his decision after hearing about the woman he'd failed to honor.

"Well," I began, carefully choosing my words, "she's very beautiful, incredibly talented on the piano, and she's kind—"

"Are you sure you're not just saying that because she's your employer?"

I smacked his arm lightly, a grin tugging at my lips. "No, I mean it. She's always been kind to me and to the rest of the staff." That much was true. But then, something deeper stirred within me, and before I could stop myself, another truth slipped from my mouth, a truth I feared I might regret later. "But, she's sad."

Graham's brows furrowed in confusion. "Sad?"

I nodded, feeling the weight of my own sorrow pressing down on me. "Yes. She feels rejected by the Duke, especially in this arrangement."

"I've met the Duke," Graham said, his tone dismissive. "Trust me, she's better off without a beast like him."

"She didn't want this wedding either. But she was willing to sacrifice her own happiness for her family, for her duty. Now, with the Duke backing out, it'll reflect badly on her. People will start to think she's the problem and the undesirable one. She may never get another chance to marry if it turns into a scandal."

"You care deeply for your lady, don't you?" Graham asked softly.

"I do," I said, "I just don't want to see her get hurt and end up living a lonely life if rumors and gossip spread about the Duke rejecting her."

Graham's expression softened as the weight of my words sank in. "I hadn't thought about that," he murmured, a shadow of sadness crossing his face. His eyes, usually so full of mischief, now held something closer to compassion. "When, or if, I see the Duke again, I'll see if I can convince him to make a public statement about why the engagement ended. Hopefully, that will spare Lady Charlotte's name from any damage."

"Thank you," I said, a wave of relief washing over me. It wasn't a complete solution, but it was a start.

"Of course," he replied simply, his gaze lingering on me for just a moment longer before he turned away.

Chapter 12: Charlotte

My muscles ached in the most satisfying way as I sank down onto the edge of the bed, letting out a small, contented sigh. The manor was finally looking as it should, clean and alive with a warmth that hadn't been there before. But after a full day of scrubbing, sweeping, and dusting every corner, I felt as though I'd aged ten years. I couldn't recall the last time I'd worked so hard, though part of me was proud of the results. Graham had even complimented me, which, if I was being honest, felt like a strange sort of victory.

I pulled my legs up onto the bed and curled into a ball, my fingers gently massaging the aching muscles in my calves. I wasn't sure how long I could keep up this pace, but for now, it didn't matter. I was tired, and all I wanted was warmth and rest. Just as I was about to let my eyes slip closed, the door creaked open, and I turned my head in surprise.

"Charm," Graham's voice called softly, as if unsure of disturbing me.

I lifted my head, blinking in confusion. "What is it?"

"I'm sorry, did I wake you?"

"No," I breathed, "but I am tired."

"I thought you might be a little sore after all that cleaning," he said, walking closer, "so I drew you a bath in the bathing room down the hall, the water is freshly heated if you are feeling up to it?"

"You... You made me a bath?" I asked, my voice a bit higher than usual, stunned by his thoughtfulness.

"Figured it might be nice to relax a little," he said, his mouth curling into an almost shy smile as he glanced at me. "You've been working nonstop. You deserve it."

I swallowed, still not entirely sure how to respond. I felt both touched and self-conscious. The idea of him going out of his way like this was foreign to me, strange, but in a good way.

"I didn't realize you were allowed to be kind on purpose," I said, my voice teasing, but there was an edge of something real in it too.

He raised an eyebrow at that, but I saw a flicker of something in his eyes. "Don't let it go to your head. I'm still making you do all the hard work around here."

"Oh, don't worry," I said with a grin, "I'm used to it by now. Besides, a bath? I think that might be worth it."

He looked at me for a beat too long, and for a moment, I felt the temperature of the room shift. The air between us crackled for a second, but he quickly cleared his throat and turned toward the door to lead me to the bathing room.

"Right. Well, take your time. I will be just down the hall if you need anything." His voice softened. "I'll leave you to it."

I nodded, grateful for the moment of solitude. Graham didn't linger, and after a few moments, I heard the faint click of the door as it shut behind him. I could breathe easier now.

With a small groan, I padded across the room to the tub. The smell of lavender and warm water filled the air, and my eyes closed involuntarily as I dipped a hand into the water. It was the perfect temperature. Comforting and soothing.

I didn't waste another moment. I shed my clothes quickly, tossing them aside, and eased myself into the tub. A deep, contented sigh escaped me as I sank into the warmth, the heat soaking into my skin, melting the tension in my muscles. I closed my eyes and let my head fall back against the edge, my hair floating just above the surface of the water.

The bath felt like it had lasted only a few minutes, though I must have dozed off because when I opened my eyes again, the room was dim. The candlesticks had burned low, and the shadows had deepened across the walls. I blinked, disoriented, as I lifted my hand to wipe the sleep from my eyes. *How long had I been in here?*

I reached for a towel nearby and quickly wrapped it around my body, then stepped out of the tub, feeling almost weightless as I moved.

As I returned to the bedroom, I noticed something that hadn't been there before. On the bed lay a beautiful green dress. The fabric was rich, smooth, and elegant, almost like it had been made for a ball or a special occasion, nothing like my worn down dress I had been wearing for days now. The color was a deep emerald that complimented my hazel eyes perfectly, and as I stepped closer, I noticed the fine stitching that ran along the seams, the delicate lace edging the neckline.

I gasped quietly, tracing my fingers over the soft fabric, still stunned by its beauty. It was the kind of dress that would make any woman feel special, and for a moment, I felt like someone else entirely, like a woman deserving of such a thing after all my lies. And then I saw it, a bushel of red wild flowers with a single rose placed delicately beside the dress. The rose's petals were soft and snow white, as if it had been chosen with great care as the centerpiece. *Where did he even get these? Maybe the greenhouse?*

There was a small note attached to the rose. I unfolded it carefully, reading the elegant handwriting:

"Meet me for dinner. —G."

I pressed the note to my chest, my heart skipping a beat. His handwriting, though simple, had a certain elegance to it. I glanced at the door, but Graham was nowhere to be found. Still, I quickly changed into the dress, the fabric feeling like silk against my skin. I stuck the rose into my hair for an accessory as I smoothed the dress down. It fit perfectly, hugging my waist and flowing gently down to the floor. I felt a little lighter, a little less like a frightened girl lost in a strange house. The rose completed the entire look and I felt a sort of satisfaction when I drank in my reflection.

As I made my way downstairs, I felt a strange flutter in my chest. I didn't know what was happening between us. I didn't know what Graham wanted from me or if he even liked me. But tonight felt different.

The room where we'd had our earlier meals was now set for a proper dinner. The table was lined with rich dishes, roast meats, vegetables, fresh bread, and wine glasses set with care. It looked like something out of a grand house party, though the soft candlelight and the crackling fire in the hearth made the space feel intimate and private.

I caught a glimpse of Graham as I entered the room. He was standing near the fire, wearing a dark jacket with the sleeves rolled up. He glanced up when he heard me approach, his gaze lingering on me just a bit too long, making my heart beat faster. For a moment, we just stood there, the space between us filled with unspoken words.

"You look..." he started, then paused, as if searching for the right words. "You look stunning."

I couldn't help but smile, my cheeks warming slightly at the compliment. "Thank you. You're not so bad yourself."

He chuckled, and waved me toward the table. "Please. Sit. I made us dinner."

The scent of the food wafted through the air, and I took a seat, already feeling a little dizzy with the anticipation of what came next. Graham poured us each a glass of wine, and we clinked glasses before digging into the meal.

It was a simple thing, but it felt incredibly special. We spoke of small things at first. How the manor had started to feel more like home, how he hadn't realized how nice it was to have company, how I hadn't imagined I'd ever be in such a place, let alone share a meal with someone like him.

As the evening wore on, the conversation grew more playful, more comfortable. And at some point, with the last of the wine gone and the fire burning low, I found myself standing and pulling him by the hand into the center of the room.

"What are you doing?" he asked with a raised eyebrow, but he didn't resist when I placed his hand on my waist.

"Waltzing," I said with a grin. "No music. Just us."

"Do maids know how to dance?"

"Do groundskeepers?" I challenged.

He laughed, shaking his head. "You're mad."

"Perhaps. But come on, just one dance," I teased, swaying slightly to a rhythm only we could hear.

And so, with no music but the crackling of the fire, we danced slowly, awkwardly at first, as if we were both testing the waters. But with each step, we grew more comfortable, our movements more natural. I felt his hand on my waist, and I placed mine on his shoulder, my fingers pressing lightly against the fabric of his jacket.

We moved around the room, the only sounds our quiet breathing and the soft hums we each contributed, lost in the moment. And at one point, as I spun, I caught the look in his eyes, the way his gaze softened when he looked at me.

I felt the distance between us close, as if the whole world had narrowed down to just the two of us in the flickering glow of the firelight. His hand was warm against my waist, and I could feel the subtle pressure of his touch, guiding me in our small waltz. I was dizzy, not from the wine, though that might have helped, but from the overwhelming closeness between us. The soft hum of our voices filled the silence, the tension rising like a pulse beneath the surface of the dance.

When I spun in his arms, the motion almost felt too fluid, like I was weightless, caught in the current of his gaze. Our eyes locked for a long moment, and for a second, everything else seemed to disappear. The world faded to just us, standing in this room, bathed in the golden light of the hearth.

"Charm," he whispered, his voice low, and I felt a shiver race down my spine at the way he said my name, soft but urgent, like it held some sort of promise.

Before I could respond, he drew me closer, the space between us shrinking even more. My breath caught, and I felt his warmth spread through me, his chest rising and falling against mine.

SHADOWS OF GRAVEWOOD MANOR

It was the smallest of movements, but our faces tilted slightly toward one another. The tension was thick, almost unbearable, and the need for some kind of resolution hovered in the air. My heart beat faster, my mind racing with questions, *what was happening between us?*

And just as I thought he might kiss me, his hand tightened briefly on my waist, and he pulled away. He stepped back, breaking the moment with a quiet, frustrated sigh.

"We need to stop," he said, his voice rougher than I expected. "It's getting late, and you... you're still recovering and we have been drinking."

I blinked, momentarily stunned, but quickly covered it with a small, forced smile. "Of course," I said, trying to ignore the ache in my chest. "I'm just glad you made dinner. It was perfect."

He didn't meet my eyes for a moment, his expression unreadable. Then, after a beat of silence, he said gruffly, "I'm just trying to do something nice for you, Charm. It's not easy for me to... let go of the things I'm supposed to do."

I nodded, though my heart ached with an unspoken longing. "I know," I said softly, "but you don't have to do it all alone."

He looked up at me then, his gaze intense, but he didn't say anything. Instead, he reached for another wine bottle and refilled our glasses. A quiet understanding passed between us.

We drank more wine, the warmth from the fire and the alcohol making me feel lightheaded in the best way. The night stretched on lazily, and we talked about everything and nothing. The laughter flowed easier now, and with each passing moment, the space between us seemed to close.

When the fire finally died down to embers and the house was quiet, we found ourselves curled up by the hearth, the wine and the quiet intimacy of the evening making me feel a sense of contentment I hadn't expected. I nestled into the crook of Graham's arm, feeling the weight of the day's work drift away.

"You should sleep," he said softly, pressing a kiss to my forehead, a gesture that both startled and soothed me. "I can take you to your room—"

"No," I quickly said, not wanting this moment to end, "I'm comfortable right here. Please don't leave."

"I'll be right here." He said and placed a gentle kiss on my temple.

When the fire finally dwindled to embers, and the soft crackling of the wood was all that remained, we found ourselves in a comfortable silence by the hearth. I felt an unexpected warmth spread through me, not just from the heat of the fire but from the presence of Graham beside me.

I had no idea how much time had passed since we'd danced, but it felt like we were suspended in some bubble where nothing else mattered. My head rested on his shoulder, his hand resting on my waist, just where it had been during the waltz.

I could feel his heartbeat beneath my palm, steady and strong. There was something electric in the way he held me, in the way his fingers traced lazy, almost absentminded circles over the fabric of my dress.

"Charm," his voice broke the silence, low and quiet, a little rougher than usual. His hand shifted, his fingers sliding a fraction lower on my back, brushing against the skin that was exposed from where my dress had slipped just slightly. "I don't know what it is about you..." His words faltered, and for a moment, I thought he might say something else, something important, something revealing. But then he cleared his throat, and his hand withdrew slightly, just enough to let the tension linger, but not enough to pull away entirely.

I swallowed, my breath catching at the sudden closeness. "What do you mean?" My voice felt foreign, thick with unspoken emotions. I could feel the heat of his body so close to mine, his warmth seeping into my skin.

"You..." He trailed off again, as if struggling to find the right words. "You make everything feel different. Like I'm not just going through the motions."

His hand returned to my waist, just a bit firmer this time, and I let out a breath I hadn't realized I was holding. "I don't know what you mean," I whispered, though the truth was, I understood completely. I felt it too, the way his presence made everything seem sharper, clearer. Like my world had become more vivid the moment he stepped into it.

His gaze dropped to my lips, and for a split second, the world seemed to pause. The air between us crackled with something dangerous, something unspoken. Slowly, he leaned closer, his breath warm against my face. I could feel the tension building between us, thickening with every heartbeat.

"Charm," his voice was barely a whisper now, his hand moving slowly, his fingers slipping beneath the edge of my dress just enough to send a shiver down my spine. "I don't think I can ignore this anymore."

My heart stuttered in my chest. I didn't pull away. In fact, I found myself leaning into him, my body responding to the heat of his touch. But just before our lips could meet, he stopped.

He pulled back ever so slightly, his forehead resting against mine as he took a deep breath.

"I shouldn't," he murmured, his hand sliding to the back of my neck, his fingers splaying wide as if he were trying to hold me in place. "I'm not...I'm not sure this is what you want, Charm."

I opened my eyes to find his face so close to mine, his pupils dilated, his lips parted. The moment felt like it was stretching, becoming unbearable.

I placed my hand on his chest, my fingertips brushing over the soft fabric of his shirt. "Don't worry about what I want," I said, my voice barely above a whisper. "I think I've known for a while."

At that, he kissed me. It was soft at first, a gentle press of lips, like a question, like an invitation. But then, something shifted. The kiss deepened, and the world around us fell away. His hand tangled in my hair, pulling me closer, and I melted against him, the heat between us spiraling out of control. His touch was urgent, hungry, but still tender, as if he were afraid to push too far, even though everything inside me was begging for more.

When he finally pulled away, both of us breathless, I could barely keep my thoughts straight. His lips hovered above mine, his breath mingling with mine in a way that made everything inside me burn.

"I didn't want to do this," he whispered, his voice raw. "I didn't want to make you feel like you had to stay."

"I'm not going anywhere," I breathed, my fingers curling into the fabric of his shirt as I pulled him back toward me.

SHADOWS OF GRAVEWOOD MANOR

But just as quickly, he paused again, his chest rising and falling beneath my palm. "I don't want you to regret this," he said softly, his voice full of something I couldn't quite place, fear, maybe. Or something darker.

"I won't," I replied, my voice steady, though my heart was racing. "I promise."

And with that, he kissed me again, this time with no hesitation, no pull-back. It was as if the moment we had both been waiting for had finally arrived, and there was no turning back. His fingers brushed down my spine, a slow, deliberate caress that made my breath hitch.

The sensation spread through me like wildfire, searing me with heat. I couldn't remember the last time I felt so alive, so attuned to someone else. I swallowed, my throat suddenly dry as his hand slid lower, grazing the curve of my waist and igniting something deep within me.

His body shifted beneath me, and before I knew it, I was straddling him, the heat of his chest pressing against mine. I could feel the hardness of him through the fabric of his trousers, and it made my pulse quicken.

His hands moved instinctively to my waist, sliding up the sides of my dress to grip my hips, pulling me even closer, if that was even possible.

"Charm," he murmured against my lips, his voice ragged. "I can't keep pretending I'm not this close to losing control."

I responded without hesitation, pressing myself into him. "Then don't," I breathed. "I don't want you to stop."

His hands were on me again, moving under the fabric of my dress, caressing the bare skin of my thighs. The heat of his touch sent a shockwave through me, and I found myself shifting restlessly against him, unable to stop the tremors that coursed through me. My body ached for more, and I couldn't help but roll my hips in time with his touch, seeking more friction, more connection.

His lips found my neck, trailing down to my collarbone, nipping at the sensitive skin, and I let out a gasp. "Graham!"

My voice was filled with desire. I tugged at his shirt, desperate to feel more of his skin, to feel the warmth of him, the rawness of him.

With his chest now bare, I felt a small hitch in my breath as I drank in his beauty. His muscled torso was hard as stone and I couldn't stop my wandering hands from exploring every inch of him. My hands had a mind of their own as they traveled further down and rested just a top his trousers that housed his hard erection.

He paused, lifting his head just enough to meet my eyes. His gaze was dark, swirling with a mixture of passion and something softer-something that made my heart thud harder in my chest. He quickly adjusted the rose in my hair, making sure it was still safely in place.

"Are you sure?" he asked, his voice barely above a whisper. His hands were still resting on the curve of my waist, his touch gentle but firm, as if he needed to know that I wasn't just swept up in the heat of the moment. "Once we go past this point, there's no turning back."

I searched his face, feeling a surge of certainty. "I've never been more sure of anything in my life."

He exhaled a breath he'd been holding and kissed me again, this time with all the intensity of everything unspoken between us. He pulled me closer, his hands roaming beneath the fabric of my dress again as I slid my hand down inside his trousers finding his hard cock. I began to stroke him in time with his lips planting kisses trailing down the column of my throat. His touch was careful, deliberate, like he was worshiping the very skin he touched. Every inch of me felt alive under his hands.

"God," he whispered, his voice rough as I picked up my stroking pace. "You drive me mad, Charm."

I laughed softly. "It's only fair. You've had the same effect on me."

His lips curled into a half-smile, but it was edged with something darker. "I don't think I can hold back much longer," he warned and threw his head back.

"I don't want you to," I whispered, my voice trembling with want.

And just like that, the distance between us seemed to vanish. He kissed me again, a claim that was both passionate and gentle at the same time. His hands moved up to my back, untying the laces of my dress with a practiced ease, and I shivered as the fabric loosened around me. He pulled it down my shoulders, exposing the bare breasts beneath, and I gasped at the cool air meeting my peaked nipples.

His gaze was burning as he looked at me, at all of me. There was no judgment, no hesitation in his eyes, just a deep, unwavering desire.

"I want you," he said, his voice thick with emotion. "I've wanted you since the moment I saw you."

I smiled, the words finally finding their way into my heart. "Then don't make me wait any longer."

He chuckled darkly and kissed me again, his hands now moving lower between my thighs, his touch teasing and possessive as he found my most sensitive spot. Every time I thought I couldn't take it anymore, he pulled back just enough to keep me on the edge, desperate for more.

But then, just as the tension between us reached a breaking point, he pulled away, his breath coming in ragged gasps. He looked at me, his eyes wide, almost pained.

"I don't want to rush this, Charm," he said, his voice strained. "I need to know you're not doing this just because you feel like you have to. I need to know you want this."

I met his gaze, "I want you," I said, my voice steady. "I want this."

He exhaled a long breath, as if he were relieved. Slowly, carefully, he lowered my back onto the couch, his lips trailing over my sensitive nipples as he held me. His hands trailed beneath my dress, his soft fingers finding that sensitive spot between my legs again.

"Graham," I moaned as his fingers moved in circular motions along the sensitive ball of nerves.

"You're so beautiful, writhing beneath me," Graham said, shooting me a wicked smile before lowering his mouth to give attention to my other breast.

I wanted him, wanted more of him. His thick cock teased me as he rubbed himself over my aching body. It was more than a want, it was a need.

"Graham," I whimpered as I felt his finger slide between my folds and into my core causing the foreign feeling to make my body jolt.

"Did I hurt you?" Graham asked, his face flushed with worry as he withdrew his finger.

"No," I grabbed his face with my palms, "please keep going."

SHADOWS OF GRAVEWOOD MANOR

Graham did as he was told and returned his finger to my entrance, pumping it in slowly at first until my body relaxed into a steady rhythm causing pleasure to burst from my core.

"More Graham," I moaned and pleaded, "don't stop!"

Before I knew it, another finger joined in, stretching me even more. The feeling was all so overwhelming. It was like nothing I had ever felt before.

"Charm," Graham breathlessly moaned as he finally withdrew his fingers from me, "I need to taste you."

I nodded and without another second of hesitation, Graham's tongue slipped between my folds where his fingers had just been. His tongue pushed into me in a circular motion before he withdrew, bringing his lips back to that sensitive bundle of nerves.

"You taste like the winter air that blew you here," Graham whispered between my thighs before returning his mouth to my core.

It was all too much but I still wanted more. I still craved more. I could feel my self- tipping over the edge, but I didn't want to, not yet. Not unless Graham was about to join me.

"I want more and I want to see all of you. I want all of you." I pleaded.

Graham entertained my request and stripped away his trousers as I peeled off my dress. We were both bare full of wanting. I let my eyes trace down his muscled torso once again, all the way down to where is cock hung low and hard. It looked even bigger than it felt in my hand.

"You're beautiful," was all I could say as I sat up and continued to drink in the sight of him.

A wicked smile formed along his glossy swollen lips. "Lay down," he commanded and I did as he asked.

My heart began to race again, understanding fully well what I was now inviting him to do. Inviting him to experience with me.

"Have you done this before?" Graham quietly asked as he hovered his body over mine.

I shook my head, hoping that my lack of experience wouldn't make him change his mind. I was too worked up and this just felt right. I had to feel every inch of him. I wanted him inside me.

"It might sting at first, so I will go slow, alright?"

I nodded as I felt him line himself up with my entrance. The head of his cock began to push inside me, causing my body to tense. I focused on my breathing to loosen myself up just in case he changed his mind in fear of hurting me. I took a deep breath and as I exhaled, he sheathed himself all the way in.

I closed my eyes tight at the pain as Graham stilled inside of me.

"We can stop, just say the word," Graham reassured me, while he grazed my neck with his fingertips.

"No," I spat out quickly before he could decide for me. "Keep going."

Graham followed my orders as he began to thrust his cock slowly in and out over and over again. After the initial pain, I started to feel something else. Something closer to pleasure as the friction began to overtake my body. I could feel a climax building again, a feeling I had only been able to give myself in my most un-lady like moments alone in my room.

"More, more," I begged as my hands grabbed at his hips urging him to move faster and deeper.

"Charm," he moaned into my ear, his hot breath tickling my neck. "I don't think I can last much longer."

I was right there with him tight rope walking along the edge. My body began to shake as I felt my climax fill every inch of me. "Graham!" I called out as I rode the wave of pleasure he was giving me.

"Oh God," Graham said as he pumped into me faster and faster, "Charm!" he shouted as he gave into his release, his climax following my own.

His body collapsed onto mine as I wrapped my hands around his trembling body. He hadn't pulled out of me yet as the two of us laid there trying to catch our breaths. I wanted this moment to last forever. I crossed a line I could never uncross, and I didn't care. This felt right, like it was always suppose to be Graham who I would first experience this with. It was as if the universe had put all the right pieces into place.

When Graham finally withdrew himself from me, I instantly missed the feel of our two bodies connected in such an intimate way. We stayed naked on the couch, too tired to make the trip up the steps to our rooms. Instead, Graham grabbed a quilt and wrapped us both inside of it as he held me in his arms.

"Charm?" Graham said like he wanted to tell me something.

"Yes Graham?"

He said nothing. He simply kissed the top of my head and squeezed me tight. "I'm glad I'm not alone."

"Me too," was all I could reply before I let the warm and safe feeling of his arms rock me to sleep.

Chapter 13: Graham

I woke to the soft sound of her breathing beside me, the rhythm slow and peaceful. The warmth of her body was pressed against mine beneath the quilt. I had never been so close to anyone, and yet, here she was, lying beside me in the dim morning light, her hair spilling across the couch.

Her face was relaxed in sleep. Her features softened, the small lines of worry that usually tugged at the corners of her mouth absent. She was beautiful, so impossibly beautiful that it felt like a cruel twist of fate that someone like me, someone who didn't deserve even a fraction of her, was the one lying beside her. The one she had chosen to experience such an intimate moment with. And I was the selfish bastard who didn't stop her.

I couldn't stop staring at her. Every inch of her skin, every subtle curve of her body, was perfect in a way I hadn't even known was possible. Her eyelashes were long and delicate and I found myself tracing the soft slope of her nose, the curve of her jaw, with my eyes. It was almost as if I wanted to memorize every part of her, afraid that if I looked away, she would disappear.

I reached out slowly, my fingers brushing her shoulder, barely a whisper of a touch. The warmth of her skin against my fingertips made my chest tighten. She didn't stir, and I let my hand linger there for a moment, enjoying the feel of her skin under my palm. I wanted to believe that this was real, that it wasn't some dream I would wake from.

I pressed my lips softly to her shoulder, just below the curve of her neck. The scent of her, something sweet and clean, like fresh lavender clung to me, intoxicating. She shifted in her sleep, her breath hitching for a bit then, she settled again, oblivious to my gaze, to the way my heart seemed to beat harder whenever I was near her.

It wasn't fair, was it? None of it.

I wasn't the man she thought I was. The truth, *my* truth, had to come out eventually. But how could I tell her? How could I bring myself to destroy the only thing I'd ever wanted? She deserved someone worthy of her, someone who could give her the life she wanted. Not someone like me. Someone broken.

I clenched my jaw, pushing those thoughts aside. It wasn't the time for regrets. It wasn't the time for thinking about the inevitable. Right now, I had her. Right now, she was here with me, and I wasn't going to waste this moment.

My lips trailed down the curve of her shoulder, the soft, silken skin under my mouth making my stomach tighten. Her scent was intoxicating, filling me completely.

What had I done to deserve this?

I shouldn't be here. I should have kept my distance, kept her at arm's length. But I hadn't. I'd pulled her closer, drawn her in, because every part of me longed for her. I had to tell her the truth. But even as the thought crossed my mind, something deeper within me begged me to wait, to hold on to what we had, even if it was just for a moment.

SHADOWS OF GRAVEWOOD MANOR

I leaned in, pressing another kiss to her shoulder, then to the back of her neck. She let out a small sigh, and my heart skipped a beat. God, I was going to lose her. I was already losing her, and I wasn't sure I could handle that. But the truth was a weight I couldn't keep carrying. I knew it was only a matter of time before it broke us both.

I shifted carefully, not wanting to wake her just yet. I wanted to savor this, *her*, this closeness, the feel of her against me. It was something I had never known I needed until it was too late to take it back. I slid my arm around her waist, drawing her even closer, as she unconsciously nestled against me.

My gaze never left her face. She was still so innocent, so unaware of the storm that was brewing inside of me.

She stirred again, a faint groan escaping her lips as she stretched her arms above her head. Her hair fanned out across the pillow, framing her face in a wild halo of chestnut curls.

"Good morning," she murmured, her voice hoarse with sleep, but the sound of it was enough to send a surge of warmth through me. She blinked her eyes open slowly, those hazel eyes of hers finding mine, her lips curving into a soft smile.

I couldn't breathe.

"Good morning," I replied, my voice gruff, betraying the emotions I was trying to hide.

Her hand found mine, intertwining our fingers, her touch sending a jolt of electricity straight to my heart. "Did you sleep well?" she asked, her voice still laced with sleepiness.

I nodded, though it wasn't entirely true. I hadn't slept, not really. Not when she was so close, not when I was so consumed by the fear of losing her.

"I did," I said, though the words felt like a lie in my mouth. "You?"

She smiled again, her lips stretching into a grin that lit up her whole face. "I did, too."

I couldn't stop myself from leaning in, brushing my lips against hers. It was soft and gentle. A kiss born of comfort, not urgency. But it made everything inside of me ache. "You should have gone to your bed," I murmured, my voice tight.

She shrugged slightly, her gaze flickering over me. "I wanted to be here," she said simply.

I let out a quiet breath, as I noticed the white rose had fallen from her hair while she slept. I picked it up and gently tucked it behind her ear before my hand slid to her cheek, cupping her face. "I'm glad you're here," I said, barely able to speak the words, but knowing they were true.

She closed her eyes, her lashes fluttering closed. "I'm glad, too," she whispered.

I had a million things I wanted to tell her, but none of them felt right. Not yet. Maybe not ever. So I stayed quiet, savoring the feeling of her against me, the peace of this moment before everything, the truth, the lies, came crashing down.

But for now, I held her. And for now, it was enough.

Chapter 14: Charlotte

The house was quieter today. The storm had passed, and the sun had finally broken through the thick clouds, casting weak light over the empty rooms of the manor. I was still stiff from the days of cleaning, my arms sore from scrubbing floors and dusting forgotten corners. Not to mention the fornication that took place last night in the bath, then again in my bed, and one more time this morning in his. Now that I had a taste of this feeling, I was addicted. With Graham everything just felt right and easy.

Focusing on the task at hand before I got lost in my lust, I spent the rest of the morning tidying the sitting room and dusting off bookshelves in the library trying to keep myself busy or else me and Graham would never have left the bedroom. We both decided it would be more productive to work on different rooms for the day to make sure we kept our hands off of each other so we could get some actual work done.

While moving to a new part of the manor, my feet carried me down a long corridor I had yet to explore. The floorboards creaked under my weight, but I hardly noticed the sound. My eyes were scanning the hall and then, I caught sight of something unusual, an odd gap between the wall and the floor.

I bent down to investigate, my heart pounding a little faster in anticipation. A small metal handle was hidden behind a long tapestry, and when I pulled it, the door creaked open with a soft groan, revealing a dark, forgotten room.

I hesitated for a moment. *Should I really be snooping around in here?* But before I could stop myself, I stepped inside. The air was thick with the scent of mildew and dust, and the room was dim, with only the faintest slivers of light seeping in from the cracks in the walls.

I looked around, blinking in the half-light, and saw piles of old furniture, abandoned trunks, and various items stacked carelessly in the corners. It looked like no one had been in here for years. But as my eyes adjusted, I noticed something strange, pushed haphazardly to one side, there were a series of portraits. The ones I assumed were missing from the walls. They were stacked in the corner as if they'd been carelessly discarded, as if no one wanted to look at them anymore.

I felt an odd chill crawl down my spine as I moved closer to one of the portraits that had seemed to be fading. It was a painting of a man, tall, handsome, with dark blond hair and sharp, aristocratic features. His brown eyes were solemn, his expression distant.

I glanced at the other portraits, and with each one I saw, the confusion in me deepened. They were all the same man, all the same person. The Duke of Gravewood, Gregory Hartwell.

The longer I stared at the faces in the faded portraits, the more the realization settled on me. Each one of them looked exactly like Graham. There was no mistaking it. The features were the same, sharp jaw, high cheekbones. The same intense gaze.

A sudden, icy realization hit me like a slap.

SHADOWS OF GRAVEWOOD MANOR

Graham. Is Graham really Gregory? Has been lying to me the entire time?

My heart lurched, and I stepped back, my breath catching in my throat. How could I have been so blind? He'd been hiding the truth from me all along. Everything, the way he had treated me, his reluctance to reveal anything about himself, his insistence that I leave, it all made sense now. He wasn't just some humble groundskeeper. He was *the Duke of Gravewood.* My would-be fiancé.

But why? Why hadn't he told me? Why had he let me believe this lie? Was it because he didn't want me to know the truth? Or was it because he didn't want me to see him as the Duke, the man I was supposed to marry? Although I had lied to him too. He didn't know my true identity and that I was his betrothed. We were both frauds, but it didn't make the sting of this truth hurt any less.

I felt a cold knot tighten in my stomach as the reality set in. How could I have missed this? How could I have been so naïve?

Shakily, I turned and walked out of the hidden room, my head spinning. I needed answers. I needed to confront him.

I made my way through the manor, my footsteps quick and sharp against the wooden floors as I searched for him, my mind racing. I didn't know how I was going to approach him, how I was going to ask him why he had lied, why he had concealed his true identity from me. How was I going to reveal to him about my lies and who I truly was? Everything was a mess.

I checked the kitchen, but he wasn't there. He wasn't in the sitting room, either. The silence in the manor seemed to swallow everything up as I moved through it, my heart thumping wildly in my chest.

Where is he?

I pushed open the door to the small library, and there he was, standing by the fire, his back to me dusting the ledge. He didn't hear me enter, but I couldn't stay silent any longer. My voice was low, but full of conviction when I finally spoke.

"Graham."

He turned, his eyes meeting mine. And for a long moment, neither of us spoke. I could see the flicker of something, guilt, perhaps, pass across his features before it disappeared behind a mask of calm. But it didn't fool me. I could see the tension in his posture, the way his jaw tightened.

"I need to talk to you," I said, my voice becoming firm. "*Now.*"

He opened his mouth to say something, but I didn't give him a chance to speak. My eyes were burning with the truth, and I couldn't hold it in any longer. I couldn't let him lie to me any more. Not after everything I had seen.

"You're Gregory," I said simply, the words heavy in the air between us. "You're the Duke."

Graham stiffened. I saw the muscles in his shoulders tense, his eyes darken with some unspoken emotion. He didn't deny it, and that was enough.

My pulse raced as I waited for him to respond, but he remained silent.

"I need to know why," I whispered, my heart beating wildly in my chest. "Why did you lie to me?"

SHADOWS OF GRAVEWOOD MANOR

For a long moment, he didn't answer, and I thought he might turn away from me. But then, his voice came low, almost regretful.

"It's complicated," he said.

And I didn't know if I was ready to hear the rest.

Chapter 15: Graham

The weight of her accusation pressed down on me harder than I expected. I had been bracing myself for a confrontation, but hearing the words from her mouth, *"You're Gregory"* felt like a slap to the face. I had been so careful, so cautious, keeping my true identity hidden from her. I didn't want her to know. I couldn't let her know the even deeper truth I was hiding.

I watched her standing there, waiting for me to respond, her eyes burning with confusion and anger, and I knew there was no escaping it anymore. She deserved the truth. But I didn't know if I could give it to her without scaring her away for good.

Taking a deep breath, I turned away for a moment, trying to collect my thoughts. The room felt too small, too suffocating. How had it come to this? The truth of my life, the life I'd kept locked away for so long was spilling out, and there was no going back.

"I'm sorry," I said finally, my voice rough with regret. My fingers tightened around the back of the chair in front of me as I struggled to keep my composure. "I should've told you. I should've told you the truth."

I glanced up at her, but her face was unreadable. I couldn't tell if she was angry or just shocked, and the silence between us made my heart pound faster in my chest. She was waiting for me to say more, to explain myself, but I didn't know where to begin.

"I never wanted to be a Duke," I added, my voice quieter now. I let out a bitter laugh, though it lacked humor. "I still don't want to be. The title, the responsibilities, the expectations, it's all a weight I can't bear. Couldn't bear. And I never asked for any of it. It was forced on me along with the arranged marriage to your Lady Charlotte."

I could see her eyes flicker with something like pity. I didn't want it.

"I was miserable, Charm," I confessed, taking a step toward her, though I still couldn't quite bring myself to look her in the eye. "When my parents made the arrangement between me and Lady Charlotte, when they told me I was to marry some perfect stranger as part of their plan to consolidate power, to preserve the family legacy, I wanted nothing to do with it. I wanted to run, to leave it all behind. I hated the idea of marrying someone I didn't know, someone I hadn't chosen. And I was so sure I would be a terrible husband. I... I didn't even know what kind of man I was supposed to be. But I couldn't escape it. I was trapped."

My fingers dug into my palms as I remembered those days, the sleepless nights, the mounting pressure to fulfill expectations I could never meet. The thought of marriage to a stranger, someone I would never know, someone who would never love me for who I truly was, drove me mad.

I took another step toward her, suddenly desperate to explain. "I know it was selfish of me, but I lied to you because I thought it would be easier this way. I couldn't bear the thought of you thinking of me as the Duke. And I couldn't stand the idea of you thinking I was to marry your Lady Charlotte."

She stared at me, silent. The tension between us was palpable, and I couldn't tell if she was processing the words or if she had already closed herself off from me.

"I didn't want you to pity me, Charm," I murmured, my voice low and strained. "I didn't want you to look at me and see only the man I was forced to be. I didn't want to be that man."

But there was more, wasn't there? More that I hadn't said. More than I dared to admit to myself.

I took a deep breath, "And then... and then I met you," I continued, and this time my voice wavered with something I hadn't expected. "And it all changed. I wasn't miserable anymore. You made me feel alive again. You were never a part of the plan, Charm. I didn't expect you to walk into my life and make me feel like I could breathe again. But now... now I'm afraid. How could I ever marry Charlotte after meeting you?"

I moved closer to her, my heart racing, the words tumbling out before I could stop them. "I don't want anyone else. I can't marry someone else, even if I'm supposed to. I can't live a life that isn't with *you*. I can't pretend to love anyone but you."

The room suddenly felt too small. The air between us was thick with the truth I had been running from, and I wasn't sure what she was thinking, whether she was angry, or whether she understood and felt the same.

I took another step toward her, my voice barely a whisper. "I didn't want to lie to you, but I didn't know how to stop. And I still don't know what to do with all of *this* and with you."

I swallowed hard, "I never wanted this to happen. I never thought I'd fall for a woman like you, someone so... so *real*," I said, the words coming out like a confession. "But now I can't imagine my life without you. And I'm terrified of what's going to happen next."

She looked at me for a long time, her expression unreadable, and I could feel the weight of my confession pressing down on both of us. I took a deep breath, readying myself for whatever she might say.

"I'm sorry," I whispered again. "I didn't mean for this to happen. I never wanted to hurt you."

The silence between us felt deafening, but I couldn't take it back now. It was all out in the open, and all I could do was wait.

Chapter 16: Charlotte

I stared at him, still processing the weight of his words. He wasn't lying. He had never wanted to be the Duke. He had never wanted to marry a stranger. But what struck me even more than the relief of his confession was the raw honesty in his voice. The way he'd spoken about *me,* like I was real, like I mattered more than anything else in the world to him. It was too much. I could hardly breathe, the truth hanging between us like an invisible weight while I was still holding onto my own truth.

I felt something shift inside me, a pang of guilt, a tug of sadness. I had kept my own secret for too long. The one thing I had been hiding from him. The truth that had started all of this.

I couldn't keep hiding. Not from him.

"Graham," I said his name softly forgetting he was actually Gregory. My throat suddenly felt tight. He didn't look at me, but I knew he could hear me, so I kept going. I had to tell him.

"I'm not just some maid. I'm not just Charm."

He froze, his shoulders stiffening at the sound of my voice. I could feel him tense, but I wasn't going to stop now. I had already come this far. There was no turning back.

"I'm Charlotte," I said, my voice trembling slightly but stronger than I expected. "I'm the woman you were supposed to marry."

I watched as his face paled. His lips parted, and for a moment, he looked as though I'd slapped him. His expression faltered, like he was trying to piece together the words I'd just said. And the look in his eyes, a mixture of confusion, disbelief, and a tinge of hurt, made my heart ache in ways I didn't know it could.

"I didn't want to marry you either," I blurted out before he could say anything. "I didn't want any of this. I never asked for this life, this marriage arranged by my parents. But I had no choice." My voice cracked, and I paused, swallowing the lump that had suddenly formed in my throat. "You don't understand, Graham. My family was going to lose everything. We were already on the verge of bankruptcy. Without that marriage, without you, we'd have been thrown out, living on the streets with nothing to our names. I had no choice. I had to marry you. That's why I came all this way, to beg the Duke, beg *you* to follow through with the marriage."

I looked at him then, searching for some kind of understanding in his eyes. There was none. Instead, all I saw was the weight of my words crashing down on him, and the realization that I had been carrying a burden far heavier than I thought.

But then something shifted in his eyes. Something soft, something almost tender.

"I didn't expect this," I said quietly, my chest aching. "I didn't expect to be here, with you, doing *this*." I waved my hand, gesturing at the warm space around us, the small moments that had turned into something more. "I didn't expect to like you let alone fall for you. I was here for one purpose and one purpose only."

He took a step toward me, but I held my hand up to stop him. I wasn't finished. Not yet.

"Don't you see?" I continued, my voice trembling but growing stronger. "You and I, this isn't how it was supposed to be. But we're here, and we've been here for a while. And maybe, just maybe, this can still work. We're not strangers anymore. We don't have to be." I searched his face, desperately hoping he'd understand, even if only a little.

"But we could," I added softly. "Maybe we could make it work. You and I, we're not so different."

There was a long pause between us. It seemed like he was weighing everything I'd just said, trying to make sense of it. And then, to my surprise, I saw something break in him. Something that had been guarded. Something that maybe had been waiting to come to the surface for far too long.

"Charm," his voice was low, a little strained, and when he spoke my name, it was as though he was trying to say something, but the words were tangled in his throat.

I swallowed hard, unsure if I could bear hearing the words that would come next.

"I never wanted to hurt you," he whispered, and I saw the guilt, raw and overwhelming, take over his features. His eyes were so filled with emotion now, so full of regret. But I wasn't sure if that was for me, or for himself. Maybe it was for both of us.

His lips parted again, but this time the words that came out were broken.

"I'm sorry. I'm sorry for everything. I should've told you from the beginning. I shouldn't have lied to you." His voice cracked, and he looked at the floor, as if ashamed of himself. But then, his gaze met mine again, and there was something in his eyes, a vulnerability I had never seen before.

"I love you, Charm. I didn't mean for any of this to happen, but I can't deny it anymore. I love you." He exhaled sharply, as if the words had drained him.

I blinked, the shock of his confession leaving me speechless. And in that moment, the weight of everything, the lies, the misunderstandings, the years of planning and expectations, seemed to collapse in on me. But there was something else now, too. Something unexpected, something new.

"You don't understand," he said, his voice faltering as emotion overtook him. "I never thought I'd be *here*, with you. I never thought I'd *want* to be with anyone, not after everything I've been through. But I want you. I want to be with you. And I don't care if it's complicated. I don't care if it's messy. I just know that I want you, but I could never have you."

Tears were threatening to spill from his eyes, and he blinked rapidly, trying to hold them back. But I could see the tremble in his hands, and the way his body seemed to shrink under the weight of the confession.

"I'm sorry, Charm," he whispered again, his voice breaking.

I was silent for a long moment. His confession echoed in my ears, settling in the pit of my stomach. But it wasn't the apology I was waiting for. No, there was something else. Something I knew he hadn't told me yet.

SHADOWS OF GRAVEWOOD MANOR

"Graham," I said softly, the words barely above a whisper. "What else?"

He sucked in a sharp breath, and I knew, in that moment, something else was coming. And then, with trembling hands, he wiped his eyes, looking at me one last time before he spoke.

"I didn't just lie about my name," he said. "There's something else I need to tell you, or rather show you. Something you might not believe."

Chapter 17: Graham

The words hung in the air like a dense fog, and I wasn't sure how much more of this I could bear. The truth had left me raw and exposed, and I could feel myself cracking open in a way I hadn't expected. It was easier for me to show Charm, to let her see it with her own eyes than to explain it.

I took a deep breath, steadying myself as I stood before her. The woman I had spent the last few days with, the woman who had slowly begun to undo the knots in my chest, was about to learn the one thing I had kept hidden.

"Come with me," I said quietly, my voice almost too soft to carry over the tension between us.

I didn't wait for her to respond. I led her out of the manor, past the stables, and down a narrow path behind the greenhouse and towards the forest. The place I feared she found that day she gathered the vegetables. The wind was still biting, the remnants of the snowstorm lingering in the air, but it didn't matter. Not anymore.

I stopped by the far corner of the estate, just beyond the overgrown hedgerows leading to the dark woods, where the earth sloped downward. There, half-hidden beneath a tangled mess of weeds and snow, stood a tombstone.

She noticed it first, her footsteps faltering as she slowed beside me.

"Why... why are we here?" she asked, her voice small and full of concern.

I didn't answer immediately. I just let her stare at it, let her read the name carved into the stone. The cold wind seemed to blow right through me, as though it could push the truth from my lips. But it was time. She had to know.

Slowly, she bent forward, her hand reaching out as if it might stop the inevitable. But there was no stopping this, no turning back.

I watched her eyes widen, her breath catching in her throat when she saw the name.

"Gregory Hartwell. Duke of Gravewood." Her voice cracked.

I nodded, and I knew, right then, she understood. She didn't understand the full weight of it yet, but she understood enough.

"Gregory Hartwell," she repeated the name, her gaze lingering on the stone as if trying to make sense of it. "But—"

"But I'm not him," I finished for her, my voice heavy with the weight of the truth. I could already feel my heart breaking. The truth always did this to me. It broke something inside me, even as it tried to set me free. "I *was* him," I added.

She blinked, her expression confused. "I don't—"

I took a breath, trying to keep my composure. "I know this is hard to believe, but let me explain." My throat tightened, and I took a step back, needing space from her. From myself. "The reason the letters stopped, the reason I disappeared from your life," I hesitated. This was the hardest part. "It was because I died."

SHADOWS OF GRAVEWOOD MANOR

Charm looked at me, then back at the tombstone, as if trying to understand how the words fit together.

"I died, Charm," I repeated, my voice shaking. "Months ago. One night I drank myself into a stupor. I couldn't take it anymore. The thought of marrying a stranger, of being a Duke, of a life I never wanted, I wasn't ready for it. I didn't want to be the man everyone expected me to be."

I paused, my breath catching in my chest.

"I went down the stairs and slipped. The very same ones you slipped on in the manor the night you arrived. I broke my neck. And that was it. That was how I died eight months ago."

Her eyes widened, her mouth parting in shock.

"But how...?" she whispered, looking back at me as if trying to reconcile the impossible.

I bit my lip, glancing away. "The moment I died, I woke up here, in this manor. And I couldn't leave. I didn't even know I was dead at first, but after a few days I began to feel myself disappear, that's when I knew. I was stuck here, tethered to the manor. I've been trapped here ever since."

Charm stepped back, as if trying to distance herself from the weight of my words. "You're a ghost?" she whispered, her voice trembling. "But we had," she took a deep breath, "you and I—"

"Yes," I nodded, the heaviness in my chest making it harder to breathe. "I am a ghost and I am unable to leave the grounds. I was unable to even touch anything physical, not until you came along. I could touch you and I didn't know how or why."

She stared at me, her eyes filled with disbelief, her face pale. "You were that ghost that night weren't you? The one that told me to get out and leave. It had frightened me so much that when I ran to leave I fell down the steps. It was you?"

"Yes," I hung my head low.

"Why did things change?" she shook her head with confusion. "How did things change?"

"I don't know, but the longer you were around the more real I became again. I thought, maybe if I could be close to you, I could feel *alive* again," I said softly, my voice cracking. "When you arrived, it felt like everything shifted. The air felt warmer. The house, the manor, started to feel like it could breathe again. I could touch things. I could touch you. *You* made me feel real again."

I closed my eyes, feeling my emotions rise. "But now, I've realized how selfish it all was. I thought I could somehow fix things but I can't. I can't do it. I can't marry you. I can't even give you the future you deserve."

Charm was silent, her eyes filled with a mixture of confusion, disbelief, and hurt. The truth was too much for her to absorb all at once.

"I never should have lied to you," I said, my voice barely above a whisper. "I'm so sorry. I've been so selfish, so miserable. I didn't want to face it. But now you know. And I can't give you the life you were promised, the life you deserve. If I had only known you were the woman I was suppose to be with, the one I was arranged to marry, everything could have been different."

The pain on her face was almost more than I could bear. I wanted to reach out, to hold her, to tell her everything would be okay. But I couldn't.

Charm's face crumpled, her eyes welling with tears.

"I should have accepted one of those many invitations you sent me, but I wasn't brave enough to face a future I did not want. A future I thought I would be condemning you to, and for that I am so sorry Charm."

"Why?" she whispered, barely able to speak through the sobs. "Why didn't you tell me sooner?"

I opened my mouth, but the words felt like stones lodged in my throat. I had no answer that would make this better. I had no explanation.

"I was afraid," I said, the truth slipping out between the cracks of my pain. "Afraid of what I might lose. Afraid of you realizing what I truly was. I couldn't lose you, not after I got to know you and fall in love with you."

Her sobs came harder now, and she turned away, stumbling back toward the manor.

"I'm sorry, Charm" I whispered, my voice breaking.

"It's Charlotte," she hissed, her voice cracking with emotion as she began to turn away.

"Charlotte," I gently said. "Please, don't go."

But she was already gone.

I stood there, staring at the gravestone, feeling the weight of everything collapse over me. I didn't deserve her. I had never deserved her.

.

Chapter 18: Charlotte

The cold air slapped my face as I ran back to the manor, my breath coming out in harsh, ragged gasps. I didn't care that the snow was beginning to fall again, that the wind bit through my cloak like a thousand icy needles. My heart was already frozen from the weight of what Graham, no, *Gregory*, had just confessed. I could barely wrap my mind around it.

A ghost. He was a ghost. How was this even possible?

How could he not have told me? How could he let me believe, let me fall into this? *Fall for him?* Especially after we? My mind drifted to the night we first made love. I didn't know what to believe anymore. My body trembled, not from the cold, but from the raw emotions building up inside me.

How could he do this to me? I thought, my fists clenched tightly at my sides. *Why didn't he tell me sooner?*

But there was that voice, that small, treacherous part of me that still wanted to understand him. Wanted to forgive him. Because despite everything, despite the lies, despite the deception, I could still feel the pull of him. *I still wanted him.* I lied to him too, so how was that any different?

I didn't know what to do. I didn't know how to feel. The words echoed in my mind, the weight of them so heavy I could hardly breathe. I swallowed hard, trying to push them away, but they stuck to me like glue, warm and dangerous.

I was in love with him. *Wasn't I?* The idea made my chest ache. How could I be in love with a ghost? How could I possibly want someone who was already dead? Someone who lied to me for days?

I couldn't think straight. My mind spun faster than my feet could carry me, and before I knew it, I was at the door to my room, slamming it shut behind me.

The sound of the bolt locking echoed in the silence, and I crumpled against the door, my knees giving out beneath me. The tears came then, hard and fast, as I slid down the wood, letting my sobs shake through me.

He's gone. He's dead. He was never real, not in the way I wanted him to be. Not in the way I needed him to be.

I buried my face in my hands, the room feeling smaller and smaller around me. The man I thought I was growing to love, the one who made me feel *seen* and *alive*, he was gone. But wait, my mind whispered, he wasn't really gone, was he? He's still here. He still exists. He's right outside that door. *Or is he?*

The thought twisted in my chest like a knife. I wanted to reach for him, to open that door and run to him, but I didn't know how to face him. He had lied to me for so long. He was never the man I thought he was.

Minutes, or maybe hours slipped by in a haze. Finally, the exhaustion that had been building since the moment I stepped into this cursed house took hold, and I collapsed onto the bed.

My body ached, every muscle sore from the emotional toll of the day, and all I wanted was to forget. To escape from all of it. But sleep didn't come easily. My mind kept returning to Graham, no, *Gregory*, to his confession. The way he said it, as if it didn't matter anymore, as if it was just something that had to be said. But for me, it felt like everything.

I closed my eyes and tried to shut out the thoughts. *I'm just tired,* I told myself. *Just sleep.* Tomorrow I'll figure this out.

But sleep didn't come. My mind wouldn't let go, and I spent the next few hours staring up at the ceiling, my thoughts racing. Suddenly, I heard a knock at the door. I flinched, my heart leaping into my throat. I didn't want to hear his voice. Not now.

The knock came again, louder this time. "Charlotte?" His voice gentle and pleading.

I gripped the sheets tightly, my fingers digging into the fabric as I tried to force myself to move. I couldn't face him. Not yet.

"I made dinner for you," Graham's voice said, muffled through the door. "It's... it's just by the door. If you're hungry, you can have it. I will leave and let you eat in peace, but please just eat something."

I didn't know how to respond. I wanted to scream at him, to tell him how much he'd hurt me, to tell him I didn't want his pity or his food. But I was too tired to do anything but lie there, the weight of his presence pushing against the door like it was right there with me. The warmth of the meal he made, the thoughtfulness behind it, felt like a cruel joke now. But I was hungry. My body still wanted it. *I still wanted him.*

I didn't move right away. I couldn't. But after what felt like hours, I pushed myself up and walked to the door, pulling it open just enough to slide the plate inside. The moment the door clicked shut again, I felt the sharp sting of disappointment. His warmth. His presence. Gone. I sat back on the bed, holding the plate in my lap, but I didn't touch it right away.

What am I doing? I asked myself, staring down at the food. *Why am I so weak? Why am I still drawn to him?*

I ate slowly, the food almost tasteless on my tongue. I couldn't focus. The silence around me pressed in. It was suffocating.

Eventually, I set the plate aside, the remnants of my dinner forgotten. I stretched out on the bed, but my mind wouldn't stop. It swirled with thoughts of Graham, no, Gregory, *him*, my ghost. The man who was never truly there.

I lay on my side, facing the door, and tried to close my eyes again. But then I heard it.

A faint sound. A thump. It was muffled, but unmistakable. It came from just outside my door.

I sat up quickly, my heart hammering in my chest. My breath caught. *What was that?*

The sound came again, slower this time, as if it were dragging its weight against the floor. I held my breath and waited, listening closely. It was soft, but it was unmistakable.

I knew immediately who it was.

It was Graham.

He was outside my door. Prepared to make the floor his bed for the evening.

I bit my lip hard, feeling a mixture of guilt and conflict twist in my chest. *Should I let him in? Should I open the door?*

I stared at the dark wood, my hand hovering over the knob. But something held me back. *He lied to me. He lied to me, and I can't forgive him yet. I don't even know if I can at all.*

SHADOWS OF GRAVEWOOD MANOR

I swallowed, my throat tight, and pulled the covers up over me. I heard him shift again, his breath steadying as if he were finally settling in for the night. And then there was silence. Just him, outside.

I closed my eyes, trying to shut out the sound of his presence, the sound of him being so close and yet so unreachable. The comfort that only his touch could bring, now seemed like a cruel reminder of everything I had lost.

I couldn't bring myself to let him in. Not tonight. Not yet.

I turned over onto my side, my body aching, and let the darkness claim me. But sleep didn't come easily, not when he was so close.

Chapter 19: Charlotte

I woke to the sound of frantic, guttural noises, a chorus of soft, tortured gasps mixed with ragged breaths. At first, I thought I was still dreaming. But then, a sharp cry split the air, and I shot up in bed, heart hammering.

It was Graham.

I knew the sound of his voice, even distorted by fear. My pulse quickened as I scrambled out of bed, my bare feet hitting the cold floor with a thud. His screams cut through the darkness, each one more desperate than the last.

He was having another nightmare.

"Graham?" I called, my voice trembling. I moved to the door and pressed my ear against the wood, listening to his desperate thrashing. "Graham, please! Wake up!"

But there was no answer. Only the sound of his body slamming against the floor, and then the floorboards creaking beneath his restless movements.

I threw the door open, half expecting to find him tossing in his sleep, caught in the horrors of whatever dream held him captive.

But what I saw, what I *felt,* was nothing like what I expected.

Graham was there, thrashing, but there was something wrong.

His body flickered, as if his very existence was warping in and out of reality. One moment, his limbs were solid, his clothes sharp and tangible. The next, he was translucent, his form distorting like a mirage. I reached out instinctively, wanting to steady him, but my hand passed straight through him, as if he were nothing more than mist.

My breath caught in my throat. His body, it was fading. Flickering between solid and spectral. I couldn't believe what I was seeing. Couldn't make sense of it. Was he, *was he*, becoming a ghost again?

The rational part of my brain screamed in confusion, but the panic rose anyway. "Graham! *Graham!*"

I reached out again, my hand trembling, and tried to shake him awake, but he remained unresponsive, thrashing violently as if he couldn't hear me.

I called his name again, but there was no response. My throat tightened, my heart plummeting in my chest. He was fading away. *He's going to disappear*, I thought. *He's going to vanish and leave me and I will be alone again.*

A cold chill swept through the room, and I knew, deep down, that I couldn't let that happen. I couldn't lose him. I couldn't lose this man, *the man I was falling in love with*.

I didn't know what else to do. My thoughts scrambled, trying to find a way to reach him. I wasn't sure why, but the next thing I did was close my eyes, gather every ounce of courage, and press my lips to his. I had no idea if it would work. If I could even touch him at all.

My lips met his with a gentle, trembling pressure, uncertain and soft. I braced myself for the cold emptiness of air, worried that I'd pass right through him. But then something unexpected happened. His lips solidified. They were real. Warm, soft, and *alive*.

I pulled back in shock, eyes wide, my heart racing in my chest. His eyes were still closed, but something had changed. The room seemed to hold its breath as the flickering stopped. His body, once flickering between ghostly and solid, became completely real again.

And then his eyes snapped open, wide and startled, his pupils dilated with shock. He blinked rapidly, his breath coming in short, startled gasps, as though he had just been yanked from the depths of a nightmare.

"Charlotte?" he rasped, voice hoarse.

I took a step back, my heart still racing, but relief flooding through me in waves. He was here. He was real again.

For a long moment, neither of us said anything. We just stared at each other in silence, our chests heaving as we caught our breath. The moment was too raw, too loaded with everything that had happened. Everything we'd been through. I couldn't make sense of it, but I didn't care. Not yet.

Graham ran a hand through his disheveled hair, sighing deeply, as if trying to find his footing after what had just happened. "I'm sorry," he whispered, his voice shaking. "I never wanted you to see me like that. To see me weak."

"Is that why you have nightmares?" I asked hesitantly, "Do you dream of slipping away?"

"Yes," Graham replied, his eyes to the ground, "I can feel my death over and over again. I can feel the emptiness that followed soon after. It's numbing and painful all at the same time."

My throat tightened. "Graham, I—"

"I shouldn't have kept this from you," he continued, his voice more broken now. "I hate that I lied. I'm so sorry. But when I'm around you, it's like I am alive again. The further you are from me, the more I seem to fade away." He reached for my hand, but I pulled away instinctively.

I wasn't ready to touch him, not yet. Not after everything. His words hung heavy in the air. *Maybe I was the key to fixing all of this, the key to saving him.* It was too outrageous to even think about.

"I'll find a way to make this right," he said, his gaze earnest, "I swear I will. I'll find a way to get your family what you need. I know I can't fix everything, but I'll make sure you're taken care of. I promise."

I stared at him for a moment, my heart still aching in places I didn't know existed. My chest ached, and my mind was clouded with too many conflicting feelings. I wasn't sure I could forgive him, not yet, but he was trying. He was still here. He was still alive, in a way.

"I appreciate that," I said quietly, my voice rough from the tears I had shed earlier. "But I'm still angry with you, Graham. You didn't trust me. You didn't even try to get to know me the two years we were engaged. I wanted to know you so badly, but you closed yourself off from me, rejected every invite and in turn rejecting me. And now I'm... now I'm *lost*."

His eyes darkened with regret, and he nodded slowly. "I know," he said, his voice hoarse. "I know. I don't deserve your forgiveness. But I want to be the man you can trust. I want to be the man you need."

I swallowed hard, unsure how to respond.

SHADOWS OF GRAVEWOOD MANOR

We stood there for a long moment, neither of us sure where to go from here. But eventually, I sighed and ran a hand through my tangled hair. "You can stay here tonight," I said, my voice soft, reluctant. "But on the couch. I can't have you in my bed right now."

He looked at me, his expression softening with understanding. "Of course. I'll stay on the couch."

I nodded, still feeling torn in a hundred different directions. "Thank you," I whispered, unsure whether I was thanking him for staying, or for the truth he had finally given me.

I turned away, walking back to the bed. "Goodnight," I murmured, barely able to look at him.

"Goodnight, Charlotte," he said quietly, his voice holding an edge of regret as he said my real name.

I lay back down, staring at the ceiling, my mind a whirlwind of confusion. I could hear him settle onto the couch, the soft rustle of blankets, and then silence.

But sleep didn't come easily. The weight of everything: the ghost, the lies, the confessions, it all pressed down on me. How could we move forward from this? How could I ever trust him again? How could I love someone I didn't fully understand?

But still, I could feel his presence. Even from across the room. And it felt *real* in a way I hadn't felt before.

Chapter 20: Graham

I sat on the edge of the bed, my hands clenched together, trying to steady the thudding of my heart. Charlotte had locked herself in her room again after I returned to mine this morning.

She had to leave. I knew that. The snow had stopped, the wind had quieted down, and the roads were finally passable. If she did not go, then it was only a matter of time that her parents came to retrieve her which would surely only make things more complicated.

She *had* to leave. There was no future for her here.

But even as I told myself that, as I thought about how much better it would be for her to go home, back to her family, I couldn't help but feel a hollow emptiness settle in the pit of my stomach. Every inch of me screamed that she belonged here, that she couldn't just walk away from me, from this place, from *us*. But that was selfish, wasn't it?

She had her life waiting for her outside these walls. A future. A future I couldn't offer her. A life she would never have if she stayed here, with me, in this empty, haunted house. What was I supposed to do? I was a ghost. A fading one at that and I would continue to fade the further she was away from me.

But Charlotte, she was real. *Alive.* She needed a future. A future that didn't involve me holding her back from living.

So, I would let her go.

The door creaked open, and there she stood, her face drawn, tired, her eyes not quite meeting mine.

"Morning," she said softly, her voice almost tentative. I hated that she felt like she had to be careful with me now, that we had to dance around everything we were, everything we'd almost become.

"Morning," I said, my voice too thick, too raw.

I didn't want to make this harder. I didn't want to make *anything* harder.

But I had to be honest with her, as much as I hated it. "Charlotte, I," I took a deep breath, "I think it's time for you to go."

Her eyes flashed up to mine. There was a flicker of confusion in them, maybe a little hurt, but she didn't say anything.

"I know it's been complicated," I continued, my throat tight as I tried to find the right words. "But you need to go. You don't belong here. You need to be with your family." I could barely get the words out. I felt like I was choking on them.

"I'll send you what you need," I said quickly, trying to hold back the surge of emotions threatening to spill out. "Money. Assets. Whatever you need to make sure you aren't hungry or homeless. I won't leave you to struggle, Charlotte. I won't."

She stared at me, her expression unreadable, and I could feel my heart breaking all over again. She didn't say anything at first, and I was afraid she wouldn't. But then, her shoulders slumped, and she looked away, biting her lip.

"I don't want to leave," she whispered, so quietly that I barely heard it.

My breath hitched at the sound of her voice. *Don't make this harder*, I begged silently.

"I know you don't," I said, my voice cracking. "But I'm not the man you think I am. And this place isn't a future I can offer you. You deserve more than that."

She stepped closer, her eyes meeting mine, and I saw something, something I couldn't quite name there. "I'm not afraid to stay. I'm not afraid of you, of what you are. I just—" She faltered, her words failing her.

"You deserve a life, Charlotte. A real one," I murmured. "Not one stuck in a house with a ghost who can't give you anything. I'd only make things worse and I could never do that to someone I loved, and I do. I love you Charlotte."

Her lips trembled, and I hated it. "Then why do you want me to go?" she asked, her voice thick with emotion.

"Because I can't be selfish."

She stared at me, searching my face for something, some answer, some explanation. But I couldn't give her one.

"I'll get your horse ready," I said, trying to break the silence, trying to break the tension building between us. I turned away from her, my chest tight with all the words I couldn't say.

I didn't want her to leave. I wanted to scream that I couldn't lose her, that I had already lost so much and couldn't bear to lose her, too.

But I didn't.

I wouldn't.

It wasn't long before I was walking beside her, leading Raven by the reins, toward the stables. She followed behind me quietly, her footsteps soft, unsure. I knew she didn't want to go.

Hell, I didn't want her to go, but this was what was best. This was the right thing to do.

We reached the stables, and I stopped for a moment to look at her. She was standing close. Close enough that I could feel the warmth of her body, but far enough that I knew she was keeping her distance. She wasn't sure anymore.

"I'll miss you," she said softly, almost too softly as if she were scared to admit it.

"I'll miss you, too," I replied, my voice breaking a little.

I reached out then, cupping her cheek, needing her to know that this, *this* meant something.

"I'm going to miss everything about you," I said, my thumb brushing across her skin. "But you need to go."

Her eyes were wet, the threat of tears there, but she didn't let them fall. She stood still as I looked at her. There was so much I wanted to say. So much I wanted to tell her, but I couldn't. I swallowed hard, trying to keep myself together. "One more thing, before you go. Just one more kiss. I need to feel your soft lips just one last time. Please."

She blinked up at me, her eyes wide with surprise. I saw the conflict there, the uncertainty. But then she nodded slowly, the slightest of movements.

"Okay," she said quietly, almost as if she was agreeing to something she didn't fully understand.

I leaned down then, my heart in my throat, and kissed her.

It wasn't just a kiss. It was everything. A kiss that held all the pain of the past few days. The confusion, the longing, the uncertainty. The love we both didn't know how to handle.

Her lips were warm and sweet, and she kissed me back, tentative at first, and then with more urgency, more need.

SHADOWS OF GRAVEWOOD MANOR

When we pulled away, I rested my forehead against hers, breathless, my fingers still tangled in her hair.

"I love you," I whispered.

Her breath hitched, and for a moment, I thought maybe she was going to say it back. But she didn't. She just hugged me.

One last time.

"I'll miss you," she said again quietly, her voice thick with emotion.

I let her go. I had to.

But as I watched her ride away, my chest ached. And with every step she took, I felt myself flickering, growing fainter, more distant. I couldn't stop it. I couldn't stop her from leaving.

But I couldn't stop myself from fading either.

Chapter 21: Charlotte

Every mile I rode, every hoof beat of my horse, felt like a nail driven into my chest. The further I got from the manor, the more my heart seemed to break. I wasn't just leaving a place behind, I was leaving *him*.

With each passing mile, I tried to keep my thoughts in check, but they swirled like a storm I couldn't control. *Why didn't you say it?* I asked myself. Why hadn't I told him what I should have said when we kissed? That I loved him.

I should have said it.

If I had said it, then maybe it would have been real. Maybe he wouldn't fade away like some half-forgotten dream. Maybe the kiss we shared would have been enough to make it all real.

But I was too afraid to make it real. Too afraid to say the words, because once they were spoken, once the truth was out there, there would be no going back. It would be forever.

And how could I love someone so much, knowing that in the end, I'd be left with nothing?

A ghost.

I pulled the reins, trying to focus on the road ahead. The memories of the time I spent with Graham, the laughter, the touch of his hand on mine, the warmth of his lips against my skin. All of it surged through me like wildfire. Every moment with him was a little piece of something precious, something I couldn't quite let go of, but knew I had to.

But then, it hit me.

Graham had said something to me, back in the manor. That he hadn't felt alive until I came. Since I arrived, things had changed. That *I* made him feel real again.

Fate had brought us together. It had to have.

Could there be a way to save him? Could there be a way to pull him from the edges of his ghostly existence, even if it was just for a little while? I didn't know how to fix it, but one thing was clear, I couldn't leave him behind. I couldn't walk away from this, from him. Not when I'd just discovered that this love, *our* love, was the only thing keeping him tethered to this world.

If there was even a chance I could save him, I had to try. But even if I couldn't, I couldn't turn my back on him now. No, I would rather have a piece of him than nothing at all.

I jerked the reins, pulling the horse hard to the side, and turned it back around, galloping toward the manor, my heart pounding as it started to race ahead of me. I didn't know what I would find when I got back. I didn't know what I could do, what could possibly bring him back from the brink of nothingness. But I knew one thing, I wasn't going to give up on him.

When I finally reached the manor, my heart sank into my stomach. The house was still, far too still. No Graham. No sign of him anywhere.

He was gone.

I rode in circles, my eyes scanning every corner of the property, praying that somehow he'd be there, waiting for me, ready to explain, ready to be with me. But there was nothing. Just the cold, empty manor that had once felt so full, so alive with the echoes of laughter, of voices, of *him*. Was I too late? Had he finally officially faded away into the vast nothingness?

I began to panic but then, I saw it.

By the far side of the property, near the greenhouse, there was a shadow. I couldn't see him clearly at first, but as I drew closer, I saw him, Graham, standing near the gravestone. His back was turned to me, his body flickering in and out of view, like a candle struggling to stay lit in the breeze.

I couldn't breathe. I kicked my horse into a gallop, and in a moment, I was off the horse and running toward him. I had to get to him.

I reached him just in time, my arms wrapping around him, turning him solid once again. I pulled him toward me, knocking him to the ground. My lips were on his before I even realized what I was doing.

"I love you," I gasped between frantic kisses. "I love you. I *want* you. I don't care if you're a ghost. I don't care if you're fading away. I want you. I'll love you in any form, for however long I can have you."

His hands were shaking as he gripped my face, pulling me down to kiss him again. I felt his lips, warm and real, pressing against mine. For a moment, it was like everything else around us stopped. Time didn't exist. There was only him.

The world seemed to crack open in that instant, like the very earth split with a deafening sound that I couldn't hear. But it was there. A flash of light, a spark of something beyond comprehension. A storm gathering in the air above us, the thunder crashing, and then—

LAUREN SANATRA

Lightning.

The bolt struck with such intensity, I felt the ground tremble beneath us. I gasped, but it didn't hurt. No, it wasn't like that. It wasn't painful. It was something else, something *alive*.

The rain started to fall, lightly at first, and then harder, but neither of us cared. Because something had changed.

He pulled back, breathing heavily, his eyes wide in disbelief. "Charlotte," he whispered hoarsely. "It worked. It's real, I'm real!"

I didn't understand, but I could feel it, too.

He was real. *Alive.*

For the first time since I'd met him, I saw him clearly, not flickering, not ghostly, but whole. *Alive.*

He cupped my face gently, his thumb tracing over my cheek. "I can feel it, Charlotte. I feel... *alive.*"

Tears welled in my eyes. "What happened? What is this?"

He kissed me again, softly, lingering, savoring the moment. "I don't know. But I think it's the power of love. We were always meant to be like this was always meant to happen."

My heart raced, my body trembling. "So, what now? What do we do?"

He smiled, the first real smile I'd seen on his face since the first day I'd arrived. "We live," he said, his voice steady, full of hope. "We *live*, Charlotte."

I could hardly breathe. But in that moment, I knew I didn't need to worry anymore. Because whatever happened, whatever came next, I would face it with him. No longer a ghost. No longer a shadow.

But *alive* and together we would truly live.

Epilogue

Winter had finally relinquished its grip on the earth, and as the first warm winds of spring began to stir the trees, the world outside Gravewood Manor seemed to breathe anew. The once-barren branches had begun to bloom, the flowers opening shyly to the sun's embrace, and the air smelled of fresh earth and promise. Inside, the manor had also come back to life. Every room, once dark and forgotten, now glittered with the shine of restoration. We were, I dared say, both restored. Gregory, no longer a ghost but a man of flesh and blood, and I, no longer a woman bound by duty, but one who had found a love that was as real as the world around us.

We had worked side by side for months, bringing this place back to its glory, and now, the preparations for our wedding were underway. The day, which once had been a business arrangement, was fast becoming something more beautiful than I had ever imagined. Our wedding, not one born of obligation, but of love. True, enduring love.

As we sat across from each other in the drawing room, a crackling fire dancing merrily in the hearth, Gregory gave a sigh, leaning back in his chair, stretching with the sort of relaxed ease he never had as a ghost.

"I suppose, now that spring is here and we are to be bound by law," he said, his voice thoughtful, "I'll have to get used to calling you Charlotte, won't I?"

I tilted my head, a playful glint in my eye. "And I suppose I'll have to get used to calling you Gregory." I smiled at the sound of his name, but there was something unfamiliar about it, something that felt just a little too new.

Graham chuckled, a low, rich sound that seemed to make the air between us shimmer. "I'm afraid it will be more difficult than that. I grew so accustomed to being Graham in your world, Charlotte. He was the better version of me, the version who fell in love with you." He ran a hand through his dark hair, a rueful smile tugging at his lips. "It's hard to think of myself as someone entirely different."

I couldn't help but tease him a little, a soft laugh escaping my lips. "Oh, I agree. I had grown rather fond of Graham, even if he was prone to disappearing on occasion."

He raised an eyebrow at me. "I suppose I was a bit of a ghostly nuisance, wasn't I?"

"Just a bit." I smirked.

Graham leaned forward then, his eyes warm, and for a moment, the teasing light in the room seemed to fade, replaced by something deeper. "But you did fall in love with me, even then, didn't you? Even when I was a shadow and a whisper, you still found me."

I felt my heart flutter, the room shrinking as I looked into his eyes, eyes that were no longer haunting but filled with real, tangible life. "I did," I said softly, leaning in, my voice lowering. "And I loved Graham, even when I was unsure if I would ever see you again. But the truth is…"

SHADOWS OF GRAVEWOOD MANOR

His expression softened, and he reached out, his hand brushing mine, fingertips warm and steady. "The truth is?"

"The truth is..." I faltered, my breath catching as I searched for the words. "You are Gregory now. And I have to let go of the ghost of him, even if I still carry a piece of that love."

Graham's lips curled into a smile. "I understand," he said, his voice tender. "But, Charlotte—what if I want to be Graham for you, just a little longer? For the woman who loved me when I had no form, no future? What if I want to keep that part of me for you?"

I swallowed, feeling the sweetness of his words stir something deep within me. "You would do that for me?"

"I would," he said, squeezing my hand gently, his gaze never leaving mine. "But only if you promise to still see me as I am now. As Gregory. Alive, and ready to spend every moment with you."

I thought for a moment, my heart quickening, before a thought came to me, playful and sweet. "Then," I said, my voice light, "I suppose I can indulge you, just this once. But only if you indulge me."

His lips parted in curiosity. "And how is that?"

I smiled, feeling the warmth of the moment wrap around me like a blanket. "I want to be called 'Charm.'" I said it slowly, letting the weight of it hang in the air between us. "Because that's who I was when I first fell in love with you, before all the complications, before the ghosts and the mysteries. Just, Charm."

His face softened, the smile on his lips transforming into something that felt like an embrace. "Charm," he repeated, testing it as though he were tasting a new wine. "I approve."

I beamed at him, my heart full. And for the first time in so long, we were truly at peace.

The wedding was fast approaching, the manor bustling with preparations, but none of the excitement, none of the frenzied activity, could quite compare to the joy I felt simply sitting here, in the quiet of the evening, hand in hand with the man I loved.

My family, once burdened by debts they could never have hoped to escape, now had a future free from worry. The estate was thriving, and Gravewood Manor, our home, was being filled with light and laughter once more.

Graham was preparing to take his place as the Duke again, but the thought of titles seemed so small compared to the life we would build together. No longer was he a man haunted by a past he could not change. No longer was I a woman trapped in an arrangement. We were free.

I rested my head against his shoulder, my fingers still intertwined with his. "I'm ready," I whispered. "Ready to start the next chapter with you."

His arm tightened around me, pulling me closer. "So am I," he murmured. "And whatever comes next, it's ours. No ghosts. No shadows. Just us."

And as the soft evening light bathed the room in golden hues, I knew that our love would carry us through every season of our lives. Together.

The wedding would be soon. But it wasn't just the wedding that I looked forward to. It was the life after, with him by my side, and no longer a ghost of the past to haunt our future. Only Graham and Charm.

Made in the USA
Coppell, TX
26 February 2026

72451293R00100